Anonymous

Twenty Fourth Report of the Diocesan Church Society of New Brunswick 1859

SALZWASSER
VERLAG

Anonymous

Twenty Fourth Report of the Diocesan Church Society of New Brunswick 1859

Reprint of the original, first published in 1859.

1st Edition 2022 | ISBN: 978-3-37512-180-8

Verlag (Publisher): Salzwasser Verlag GmbH, Zeilweg 44, 60439 Frankfurt, Deutschland
Vertretungsberechtigt (Authorized to represent): E. Roepke, Zeilweg 44, 60439 Frankfurt, Deutschland
Druck (Print): Books on Demand GmbH, In de Tarpen 42, 22848 Norderstedt, Deutschland

TWENTY FOURTH REPORT

OF THE

DIOCESAN CHURCH SOCIETY

OF

NEW BRUNSWICK,

1859.

INCORPORATED BY ACT OF PARLIAMENT,

16 VICTORIA, CAP. IV., 14th APRIL, 1853.

SAINT JOHN, N. B.
PRINTED BY BARNES AND COMPANY,
54 PRINCE WILLIAM STREET.
1859.

OFFICERS OF THE SOCIETY.

PRAYERS OF THE SOCIETY.

—

BEFORE THEY COMMENCE BUSINESS.

PREVENT us, O Lord, in all our doings, with Thy most gracious favour; and further us with Thy continual help; that in all our works, begun, continued, and ended in Thee, we may glorify Thy holy name, and finally, by Thy mercy, obtain everlasting life, through Jesus Christ our Lord.—Amen.

O GOD, from whom all holy desires, all good counsels, and all works of piety and charity do proceed, we beseech Thee to visit with Thy favour our Sovereign Lady Queen Victoria, and so rule her heart, that she may in all things seek Thy honour and glory. Prosper with Thy blessing the designs of this Society. Comfort with Thy grace those benefactors who contribute to its support. Bless the ministry of Thy servants, the Clergy; the endeavours of all who are engaged in spreading the knowledge of true religion in the dominions of our Sovereign, and the labours of those missionaries who are promoting the same in this Province. And may Thy Holy Spirit direct all our consultations to the advancement of Thy glory and the good of Thy Church, through Jesus Christ our Lord.—Amen.

O MERCIFUL GOD, who hast made all men, and hatest nothing that Thou hast made, nor wouldest the death of a sinner, but that he should be converted and live: have mercy upon all Jews, Turks, Infidels, and Heretics, and take from them all ignorance, hardness of heart, and contempt of Thy Word; and so fetch them home, blessed Lord, to Thy flock, that they may be saved among the remnant of the true Israelites, and be made one fold under one Shepherd, Jesus Christ our Lord, who liveth and reigneth with Thee and the Holy Spirit, one God, world without end.—Amen.

OUR FATHER, which art in Heaven, Hallowed be Thy name. Thy Kingdom come. Thy will be done in earth, as it is in Heaven. Give us this day our daily bread. And forgive us our trespasses, as we forgive them that trespass against us. And lead us not into temptation, but deliver us from evil; For thine is the kingdom, and the power, and the glory, for ever and ever.—Amen.

WHEN THE BUSINESS IS ENDED.

The grace of our Lord Jesus Christ, and the love of God, and the fellowship of the Holy Ghost, be with us all evermore.—Amen.

CONSTITUTION OF THE SOCIETY.

I.

The Society shall be called the DIOCESAN CHURCH SOCIETY OF NEW BRUNSWICK.

II.

No alteration shall be made in the Constitution of this Society, nor shall any Bye-Law, Rule or Regulation of the Society be repealed, annulled or altered, except at a meeting of the General Committee, by the vote of at least two-thirds of the members present, nor until it shall have received the sanction of the Lord Bishop of the Diocese, which sanction must be given in writing, and delivered to the Secretary, within six months of the said Meeting.

III.

No alteration or amendment in the Constitution, nor any repeal, cancellation, alteration or amendment of any Bye-Law, Rule, or Regulation of the Society, shall be proposed or made at any Meeting, unless notice shall have been given in writing at the next previous Anniversary Meeting of such proposed repeal or cancellation, nor unless the terms of such proposed alteration or amendment shall have been stated in writing at such previous Meeting; from which, without the unanimous consent of the members present, no deviation, except of a mere formal nature, shall be permitted.

IV.

No repeal, cancellation, alteration, or amendment, shall be proposed, except by a member qualified to vote at the Anniversary Meeting, whose name shall be entered on the Minutes, by the Secretary, together with the said proposition.

V.

The payment at any one time of a sum not less than Ten Pounds, shall constitute a Life Member; and the payment annually of any sum, however small, shall constitute the person paying the same, a Member of the Society. Provided that no Member shall be qualified to vote at any General Meeting of the Society, unless of the full age of twenty-one years, nor unless he be a Life Member, or shall have subscribed and paid at least Five Shillings during the year preceding such Meeting.

VI.

(Officers.)

1. The Officers of the Society shall be a President, two or more Vice-Presidents, a Treasurer, one or more Secretaries, and two Auditors of Accounts.

2. The Lord Bishop of the Diocese shall be the President of the

Society, and the Archdeacon the Senior Vice-President; and any Life Member may, at any Anniversary Meeting, be elected a Vice President of the Society.

3. The Treasurer, Secretary, or Secretaries, and the Auditors, shall be annually elected at the Anniversary Meeting; and in case of the death, resignation, or removal from the Province, of any such Officer, the vacancy shall be filled up by the Executive Committee, at its next or any subsequent Meeting within the year; and the Lord Bishop shall, if he see fit, call a Special Meeting of the Executive Committee, for the purpose of filling any such vacancy.

VII.

(*Executive Committee.*)

1. There shall be also an Executive Committee, to be composed of the following Members, viz.:

The Officers of the Society as provided for in the next preceding Article.

All Clergymen resident in the Diocese, duly licensed by the Lord Bishop, and Subscribers to the Society.

And twenty-four Lay Members of the Society, being Life Members, or Annual Subscribers of at least One Pound; to be annually elected at the Anniversary Meeting, provided that no Annual Subscriber shall be qualified to be elected, unless he shall, during the year preceding each Meeting, have paid his subscription of at least One Pound.

2. Five Members of the Executive Committee, three of whom to be Laymen, shall form a Quorum.

3. The Executive Committee shall meet either at Fredericton or Saint John, on the first Wednesday in January, on the day next following the Annual Meeting, on the first Wednesday in March, on the first Wednesday in June, and on Wednesday after the first Tuesday in October.

VIII.

(*Objects.*)

The Society shall embrace the following objects, and none other, viz.:

1. Missionary Visits to places where there is no settled Clergyman, and aid to new and poor Missions.

2. The establishment of Divinity Scholarships at King's College, Fredericton; and assistance, where necessary, to those who may be under preparation for the Ministry, especially Sons of Clergymen.

3. Aid to Sunday and other Schools in which Church principles are taught, and the training and encouraging of Schoolmasters and Catechists.

4. The supply of such Books and Tracts as are on the Catalogue of the Society for Promoting Christian Knowledge, and none other.

5. Aid to the building and enlarging of Churches and Chapels.

6. Aid to the building of Parsonage Houses.

7. The creation of a fund towards the augmentation of the stipends of Clergymen who are poor; and towards the education of the Children of such Clergymen; and towards the making a provision for those who may be incapacitated by age or infirmity.

8. The creation of a fund for the Widows and Orphans of the Clergy.

IX.

The Society will employ no Clergyman on Missionary services without the Bishop's license and appointment, and will submit its choice of Divinity Scholarships to his Lordship's approbation.

X.

It shall be competent to any Member of the Society to limit his subscription to any one or more of the objects above recited, which he may be most anxious to promote.

XI.

(*Local Committee.*)

1. The Members of the Society in each Parish, or in each Mission, consisting of two or more Parishes, shall, at the discretion of the Missionary of such Mission, constitute a Local Committee; and so also the Members residing in any District of a Parish set off under the authority of the Lord Bishop, with the concurrence of the Rector and Church Corporation of such Parish (there being in such District a Church duly consecrated, and a resident Clergyman licensed thereto by the Lord Bishop), may, at the desire of such Clergyman, and with the approval of the Bishop and the Rector of the Parish, form a separate Local Committee; and in that case the District shall, for the purpose of the Society, be considered as a separate Parish.

2. Each Local Committee shall hold an Annual Meeting on some convenient day, previous to the Anniversary Meeting, when the recommendation of the General Committee of special objects shall be determined on.

3. Each Local Committee shall be empowered to depute two Lay Members of the Society to be elected at the Annual Meeting of the Committee, to assist the Missionary in submitting the recommendations of the Committee to the consideration of the General Committee.

4. It shall be competent to each Committee to recommend any of the above recited objects to the special consideration of the General Committee, in the appropriation of the funds of the Society.

XII.

1. The Society shall hold its Anniversary Meeting at Fredericton and Saint John alternately, on the first Thursday in July in each year.

2. A Special General Meeting may be called at any time by the

President, or in his absence, by any two or more of the Vice-Presidents, four weeks notice being first given thereof by advertisement in one or more newspapers, published in Fredericton and Saint John respectively.

XIII.
(*The General Committee.*)

1. The General Committee of the Society shall be composed of the following Members, viz. : The Lord Bishop of the Diocese, who shall be the Chairman ; but in the absence of the Lord Bishop, the Committee may elect a Chairman, the Secretary or Secretaries who shall also serve in that capacity at the Meeting of the General Committee, the Treasurer and the Auditors, the Rector or Missionary of each Parish, or of a Mission comprising two or more Parishes, and the Clergyman of any separate District of a Parish (provided that in the absence or sickness of the Rector of any Parish, the duly licensed Curate or Assistant Minister shall be considered *pro hac vice* a Member of the General Committee), and the Lay Deputies elected by the Local Committees as before provided ; all such persons being Subscribers to the Society.

Proof of the election of such Deputies by each Local Committee, to be the Certificate of the Chairman or Secretary thereof.

2. The General Committee shall meet on the two days next previous to the Anniversary Meeting, to make the Annual appropriation of the funds of the Society ; and a Report of the proceedings of such Meeting shall be made at the Anniversary Meeting.

3. The Order of Business in General Committee shall be as follows:

Firstly. Production of Certificate of Lay Deputies.

Secondly. Secretary's Report to be read, and also a Report of the proceedings of the Executive Committee for the past year.

Thirdly. Report of the Auditors to be read and laid before the General Committee.

Fourthly. Such appropriations or disposition of the funds to the objects of the Society as a majority of those present may determine.

XIV.

The Clergy are requested to preach annually two Sermons in their respective Churches, with a collection on each occasion for the General Purposes of the Society.

REPORT.

For many years past, the Society has been called to consider the propriety of a change in the season for holding its Anniversary Meetings. This question, wisely referred to the Local Committees, has at length been decided. A large majority of the Lay Delegates, at the last Meeting of the General Committee, resolved upon the change. By an Act of the Legislature, published in the Appendix of the last Report, that decision has been confirmed. We meet together now for the first time, under this new regulation, and it is hoped, that the objections urged against the change, may be obviated, and that all parties will work together, in giving increased efficiency to the operations of the Society.

The Society has good reason to be thankful for the success vouchsafed during the year closed at the last Anniversary Meeting. It was a period of great difficulty and commercial depression, and yet, the contributions considerably exceeded those of any former year; and it will be found, on reference to the Treasurer's Accounts, that there remains a large cash balance, after providing for the last annual appropriations.

Considering the short time since the last Report was furnished, it was not thought desirable to call upon the Missionaries for their usual returns, shewing the duties performed in their several missions. The work is, meanwhile, going on, but more laborers are required. It will be seen by many of the reports that Missionaries are earnestly desired.

Since our last meeting, death has taken one from our number. The Rev. C. G. Wiggins, the late devoted Missionary at Greenwich and Petersville, seeking in change of climate for restoration to health, found a grave in a distant land. God has thus been pleased to deprive the Church of one admirably fitted for the Missionary work.

The Society has also of late sustained another heavy loss, by the lamented death of George D. Robinson, Esquire, for many years one of the Auditors. Ever ready to take an active part in the work and to afford assistance in the kindest and most judicious way, the removal of Mr. Robinson has left a blank which cannot readily be supplied.

The Society will be gratified to learn that a considerable addition has been made to its future resources, by a donation from an earnest minded churchman, who desires that his name may not be mentioned. This generous gift consists of a Policy of Insurance, No. 2,467, in the American Temperance Life Insurance Company, of Hartford, Conn., for the sum of $1000 ; which has been assigned to the Society, and placed in the hands of the Chairman of the Loan Committee.

To provide for the appropriations required at the present time, the members of the Society have been, in most instances, called upon for a half-yearly contribution. The result will be gathered from the following abstracts from the Reports of the Missionaries and Local Committees.

ANDOVER.—Rev. J. S. Hanford begs to thank the Society for the grant of books to his mission, and if similar appropriations are made at the present meeting, he wishes to be remembered. The collection, Mr. Hanford regrets, is not as large as that made last winter, but on the next occasion, he trusts it will be equal, if not greater, than any previous one. His efforts will not be wanting to make it so. Contributions are as follows:—Aged Clergy Fund, £2; Widows' and Orphans' Fund, £1 ; General Purposes, £13 19s; total, £16 19s.

BATHURST, SALMON BEACH, NEW BANDON, &c.—Rev. C. F. Street has forwarded an interesting report, which did not reach the Secretary in time to lay before the General Committee. Mr. Street writes, that many changes have taken place during the past six months in his mission. "Some have ceased to be members of the Church militant here on earth, but he trusts their faith has been lost in sight, and their hope in joy. Since my last report, I have found out a few other members of the Church scattered about the country.

* * * * * * * *

"I visited Point Miscou and Shippegan last March ; those Islands are more difficult of access, and more remote than any other portions of this mission, and more excluded from religious advantages. Point Miscou is about ninety miles from Bathurst. It and Shippegan are sometimes more accessible in winter, as the ice affords a bridge. The inhabitants are generally at home at this season. There are only a few families resident on these Islands, but when all assemble together, they form quite a congregation—they are most attentive to the service, and seem rejoiced to have an occasional visit from a clergyman. As some years have elapsed since these Islands were visited by a clergyman, my services were particularly acceptable."

"I have also," the Missionary adds, "visited the country below Bathurst, and most desirable it is, that Divine service should be held more frequently in Carraquet, Shippegan, &c., than at present is possible. No change can take place in this respect, till more laborers are sent to aid me in my work.

"Every month during the winter, I extended my visits to the Flat Lands ninety miles from Bathurst, also visiting the Canada side of the Restigouche."

Contributions are as follows:—Bathurst, £10; Dalhousie, £1; Salmon Beach, £1 1s. 10½d.; New Bandon, £1 6s. 4d. ; Carraquet, £3 3s. 1d. ; Flat Lands, 5s. ; total, £16 16s. 3½d.*

This amount would have been increased, if the Missionary had had time to visit lately the remote districts of his mission. They are all becoming deeply interested in the progress of the Society.

Mr. Street has also inclosed resolutions passed at a meeting of the Local

* This amount has since been increased to £18 1s. 10d.

Committee, expressive of a high appreciation of the work of the Society, and of gratitude for the aid rendered to this mission. The Committee also earnestly solicit aid toward the support of another Missionary in this very extensive district.

BLACKVILLE AND NELSON.—Rev. W. Cruden has remitted to the Treasurer £12 3s. 5d., as contributions from this mission. This, he is happy to say, is a considerable increase over the amount forwarded last year. At the meeting of the Local Committee, resolutions were passed, thanking the Society for the grant of books, and requesting another appropriation, and also asking for assistance towards repairing the Church in this mission.

CAMPOBELLO.—Mrs. Robinson has enclosed £7 7s. 6d., as the contributions from this mission.

CANTERBURY.—Rev. Thomas Hartin, on behalf of this mission, returns thanks for the grant towards his stipend, and also for the books and the renewal of the grant towards the completion of the Church.
"There is," Mr. Hartin writes, " a numerously attended Sunday School in the vicinity where the Church is erected, quite destitute of books. I do earnestly solicit a special grant for that purpose."
Contributions are £8 5s. 2½d.

CARLETON.—Rev. F. Coster reports £5, contributions from this Local Committee.

CHATHAM.—Rev. S. Bacon has inclosed resolutions passed at the Annual Meeting of this Committee, expressive of their conviction of the vast importance of the Diocesan Church Society, which they trust will be evinced by the amount of their contributions. They also thank the Society for the grant of books.
Contributions are £24 10s.

DOUGLAS.—Rev. G. Goodridge Roberts writes—"I am happy to say, as far as I can judge, the generality of my parishioners take an increasing interest in the welfare of their immortal souls, and also in the Church of which they are members.
" The attendance at my Church does not at all diminish, and I have had a few additions to the number of my communicants. The repairs to the Parish Church are almost completed, and have made a great improvement. The Tay Creek Church will, I hope, be ready for consecration before the end of the year."
Mr. Roberts requests a grant in aid of this Church, but, unfortunately, his application did not reach the Secretary till after the adjournment of the General Committee. He reports contributions for the half year, £18 8s. 9d., which he thinks exceedingly encouraging.

FREDERICTON.—The amount reported from this Parish, is about £87. Further contributions are anticipated.

GAGETOWN.—Rev. J. Neales reports contributions to the amount of £14. Mr. Neales writes, that " the alteration in the time of the General Meeting, bringing the collections so close together, has made the work more difficult, and I thought it advisable to take up only a half year's subscription on this occasion, and we have therefore improved, you see, on last year."

GLENELG, NEWCASTLE, &c.—Rev. J. Hudson reports that the Committee of Glenelg, a thinly populated Parish, met on the 11th June, and that the unfavorable weather prevented many persons from attending on the occasion ; but, he adds, those who were present, expressed by a resolution unanimously adopted, that their confidence in the general management of the Diocesan Church Society continued unabated, and that the hard times alone prevented them from increasing their contributions for the advancement of its excellent objects. The Missionary also states that an endowment fund is now being formed for St. Andrew's Church, Newcastle, and that the offertory received in the Church on Trinity Sunday last for this purpose, amounted to £7 11s. 7d. The sum of £55 has already been collected and invested towards this fund.

Mr. Hudson hopes that it will soon be in his power to remit further contributions; those just forwarded, are as follows:—Newcastle, £4 1s. 8d.; Glenelg, £2 14s. 3d.; arrears from the same Parish, £2 6s. 3d.; sale of books, £2 5s. 7d.; total, £11 7s. 9d.

GREENWICH.—J. L. Wilmot, Esquire, has inclosed the sum of One Pound Ten Shillings for the General Purposes of the Society.

"I regret very much," Mr. Wilmot writes, "that we have not been in so favorable a position for collecting as formerly. The continued absence of a minister tends to damp our energies, and the bridge, which is the principal means of communication with the lower end of the parish, having been carried away by the ice last spring, hinders our meeting together as conveniently as formerly. I, however, think I may venture to promise a further amount by the middle of October, as the most friendly and grateful feeling towards the Diocesan Church Society prevails in this Parish."

HAMPTON.—Rev. W. W. Walker reports £11 14s. 3d. as the contributions from this parish. Mr. Walker writes, "I always regretted the change in the time for holding the meetings, and the result proves that my fears were not groundless. The half yearly collections made at this season are larger than usual, and this is proof, if proof were wanting, that the people still desire the welfare of the Society."

HARVEY AND HOPEWELL.—Rev. H. Nichols reports the sum of £4 15s. already collected for the Society, and that without doubt £10 more will be added before the close of the year.

At the annual meeting of the Local Committee a resolution was passed expressive of thankfulness for the increased usefulness of the Society, and the additional support it was receiving from its members.

At Hopewell Hill, an eligible site has been obtained for a Church—the frame is being proceeded with, and the work will be finished as soon as means will allow.

At Salmon River, also, in the Parish of Alma, a site has been promised for a Church. About £40 has been raised among the people. The Missionary lately administered the Holy Communion at this place, in a small and uncomfortable school house. There are at least ten communicants in the Parish of Alma. The people earnestly ask aid of the Society to build their Church.

During the last winter, the Missionary held service at Point Wolf, five miles from Salmon River. The country here he represents as being rocky and mountainous. He is always hospitably entertained by Mr. Gideon Vernon, at whose house Divine Service is held. Many come from a distance to be present, and hear the word of God. Mr. Nichols intends visiting this place occasionally, though, in doing so, he has to travel twenty-five miles from his place of residence.

Assistance is also needed, Mr. Nichols writes, at Mechanics' Settlement, in the Parish of Elgin, on the road to Sussex. Mr. Benjamin Dowling has given four acres of land in the heart of the Settlement, and with others, has subscribed towards building a Church. Some new settlers belonging to the Church have lately arrived, and all unite in asking assistance in the work they have undertaken. The distance from the Church at New Ireland, is fifteen miles, and from Hopewell, twenty-four miles.

Mr. Nichols has also an appointment for Divine Service on the Demoiselle Creek road, on his return from the Mines, making occasionally a third service on the Sunday. The attendance here is good.

At the Mines the attendance is not so large as formerly. During Lent, the Missionary delivered a course of lectures in the week on the distinctive doctrines of the Church, which, he trusts, was productive of benefit.

KINGSCLEAR.—Rev. J. Black has inclosed a list of subscriptions amounting to £8 4s. 9d.

KINGSTON.—Rev. W. E. Scovil reports contributions to the amount of £22. He writes that "the list of subscribers rather exceeds that of last January. There has been only one collection in the Church, in consequence of the change in the time of making the returns." "It is not convenient," Mr. Scovil adds, "for me to attend the meetings of the Society this week, as they interfere with my monthly appointments for holding Divine Service at out stations."

LANCASTER.—H. Garbutt, Esquire, writes that the amount of contributions from this mission is £19, which proves, he says, that the good feeling to our Church is yet strong with us. "The want of a clergyman," Mr. Garbutt continues, "is very much felt here, not having had one here since Easter last. I hope we may soon have one, as the love of many is waxing cold. My brother warden, Mr. Carman, has been unwell for some time, but the Church here has been opened every available opportunity, the prayers read, and occasionally a printed sermon."

MAUGERVILLE AND BURTON.—Rev. A. V. G. Wiggins, D.D., has enclosed returns as follows:—Maugerville, £9 17s. 6d.; Burton, £10 10s. 8¼d.; total, £20 8s. 2¼d., which exceed the contributions of last year.

MONCTON.—Rev. W. N. Boyer has remitted £7 10s. to the Treasurer.

NORTON.—Rev. E. A. Warneford reports £19 9s. 10d., for the General Purposes of the Society.

PRINCE WILLIAM, DUMFRIES, MAGUNDY, &c.—Rev. Philip Wood Loosemore reports the sum of £24 for the General Purposes of the Society.

PORTLAND.—Rev. W. Harrison reports £44 10s., as the contributions from this Parish, and regrets that he cannot be present at the meeting of the Society.

PORTLAND, ST. PAUL'S.—Rev. Charles Lee has enclosed returns, shewing the amount contributed to be £51 8s. 3d.

QUEENSBURY.—Rev. W. H. Tippett writes that he has not quite finished his collections, which will amount to £8 or £9.* Mr. Tippett finds much hindrance in his work, from the few members of the Church living at a distance from each other. "My whole flock," he writes, "if assembled in one spot, would only form a very moderate congregation, according to city estimate, but their circumstances render this impossible, and I can only gather them together in *small* groups, at *many* points. Unfortunately, I find another drawback arising from the spiritual slumber in which too many are contented to live: this shews itself in irregular attendance at the stated public worship; in habitual absence from the Lord's table; in small and irregularly paid contributions to Church funds, and in a general want of hearty co-operation with their more earnest brethren.

*　*　*　*　*　*　*　*

"Mrs. Tippett has regularly managed a little Sunday School at the Parsonage during nine years, and I have been able to catechise the children frequently at the Sunday service, held at a school house near at hand, during the last year."

While in England, Mr. Tippett received a set of Church books for his new Church, from the Society for Promoting Christian Knowledge, and also (chiefly among his friends) he collected sufficient money to complete the work.

RICHIBUCTO.—Rev. N. A. Coster reports the amount of the half-yearly collection in Church to be £2 12s. He writes that "in speaking to the principal subscribers, it was determined to defer calling for subscriptions to the Society till Christmas, as all the collections for other Church purposes were made at the present season."

SACKVILLE AND DORCHESTER.—Rev. T. N. DeWolfe reports contributions from Sackville £7 13s. 2¼d., and from Dorchester £7 11s. 11¼d., total £15 5s. 2d.

* The subscription list since forwarded, amounts to £7 14s. 3d.

St. Andrews.—George D. Street, Esquire, Secretary of this Local Committee, reports £35 15s. for the General Purposes of the Society. A much larger sum would have been contributed but for the present depression in all kinds of business, caused by the temporary suspension of the works connected with the Saint Andrews and Quebec Railway. It is also to be noticed, that the parishioners are now, for the first time, called upon to make up a great portion of the Rector's stipend, and are at the same time engaged in building a new church and parsonage.

At the meeting of the Local Committee held on the 9th of June, the attendance was very large, and the proceedings were of unusual interest. Most impressive addresses were delivered by the Rev. H. Pollard of Saint Stephen, on the subject of our own missions, and by the Rev. William S. Chadwell of Eastport, Maine, on missions to the heathen.

Resolutions were passed expressive of a determination, both as a duty and a privilege, to further the objects of the Society, and of deep interest in the efforts now being made both in Great Britain and America for the spread of the Gospel in those countries where of late a door has been specially opened, which, in the opinion of the meeting, should at least form an object of the prayers of all who seek for the extension of the Redeemer's kingdom on the earth.

Saint David and Saint Patrick.—Rev. J. S. Thomson reports a contribution of £5 from his people, and hopes to get an additional amount.

Saint George and Pennfield.—Rev. J. M'Givern reports contributions from Saint George, £9 0s. 7½d., and from Pennfield, £1 1s. 10¼d.; total, £10 2s. 6d. He incloses a resolution passed at the meeting of the Local Committee, asking for a grant of books. The amount received for the Society, Mr. M'Givern writes, is quite as much as he could have expected under all the circumstances.

Saint John, Saint Marks.—C. H. Fairweather, Esquire, Secretary of this Committee, reports contributions to the amount of £97 13s. 10d. "I have merely to remark," Mr. Fairweather writes, "that the amount is slightly less than that forwarded last winter, which is in consequence of the subscriptions having been called for within so short a period : part of the subscribers having given half their usual contributions. I have, however, every confidence that on the recurrence of another annual subscription, the amount will fully reach or exceed that of any former year. Our present list exhibits the pleasing feature of having quite a number of new subscribers, who have cheerfully met the call made upon them for their assistance in carrying on the work of the Diocesan Church Society."

Saint John, Trinity.—A. W. Savary, Esquire, Secretary of this Local Committee, has inclosed returns as follows :—Widows and Orphans' Fund, £5; General Purposes, £230 5s. 5d.; total, £235 5s. 5d.

"When," Mr. Savary writes, "we recollect that only half a year has elapsed since the parties were called on for a year's subscription, and that only one collection in Trinity Church is included, and bear in mind the continued scarcity of money, and commercial depression, we do not see any ground for apprehending a diminution of interest in the cause. On the contrary we have much reason for encouragement in the cheerfulness and alacrity with which the subscriptions have been given."

St. John, St. James.—H. W. Frith writes, that the contributions from this Parish will not fall short of £75, and may exceed that sum.

St. Mary's.—Rev. W. Jaffrey reports £5 14s. 3d., contributions from this mission.

St. Stephen.—Rev. Skeffington Thomson, L. L.D., regrets that the approaching visitation in Fredericton will prevent his being present at the meeting of the Society. He will, however, be present in spirit, and fervently pray that the Great Head of the Church will direct all its measures to His glory, and give increased success to the Society.

"The Local Committee of St. Stephen met," Dr. Thomson writes, "at the time of the meeting of the Deanery at St. Stephens. The addresses on that occasion awakened a warm interest in favor of the Society, which will, I hope, be shewn in an increased subscription list."

Resolutions were passed expressive of thankfulness to God for the hitherto wonderful success He has been pleased to grant to the Diocesan Church Society, of confidence in the wisdom of its management, and of the hope that it will be rendered more and more effective as an instrument for diffusing true religion to the spiritually destitute places of the land, and thus in some degree replacing the gradual withdrawal of the fostering care of the venerable Society for the Propagation of the Gospel, rendered necessary by the vast field for Missionary effort opened by the Providence of God.

Contributions, not yet made up, will, it is thought, exceed those forwarded at the last meeting.

SIMONDS.—Rev. George S. Schofield has inclosed returns amounting to £4 10s. 9d. "Having had charge of the Parish only three months," Mr. Schofield writes, "I am not in a position to present a long report. I have conducted Divine Service every Sunday (with the exception of one), and on several occasions have spent part of the week in domestic visitation. As my predecessor still retains the chaplaincy of the Penitentiary, I have hitherto been able to devote all my time to the Mission, and consequently have, for about two months past, held two services on the Sunday.

"We have commenced a Sunday School at Black River, under very encouraging circumstances: about 30 young persons attend. A Library there is required, and I am requested to ask for a grant of Bibles.

"The attendance at Church is very encouraging, and I trust, by the blessing of God, the spiritual profit of the Church will be secured."

SPRINGFIELD.—Rev. C. P. Bliss is sorry that he cannot state the exact amount of the contributions, which are not yet completed. It will not, however, he writes, be less than last year.

SUSSEX.—Rev. T. M'Ghee writes as follows:—"We sincerely thank the Society for the grant for books for this mission. It has been taken up in Prayer-books, Testaments, &c. We shall be thankful for a renewed grant. We also thank the Society for the grant to the Church at the Dutch Valley. Encouraged by the latter, our contributions for this (semi) anniversary, are more than double those of the few years past. Will not, therefore, the Society give us £15 this year towards the completion of the Church of the Portage? A strenuous effort is now being made to finish that Church, which cannot be used in winter. It is eighteen miles from the Parsonage, and can only be attended every third Sunday. The congregation, on an average, is about ninety, and express great desire that I could attend them more frequently; but, being one of four Churches, widely separated, their wish cannot be complied with."

The contributions, including a collection in Church of £3 10s., will be about £22, for the General Purposes of the Society.

UPHAM.—Rev. W. H. DeVeber reports £25, contributions from this Parish, and hopes for an increased amount before the list is completed.

WOODSTOCK.—Rev. S. D. Lee Street has inclosed contributions to the amount of £7 14s. 8d., and a resolution passed at a late meeting of the Local Committee, expressive of regret that the unprecedented scarcity of money prevented additional subscriptions. The Committee pledge itself to renewed exertions, in order that such an amount may be obtained previous to the next Annual Meeting, as may, in some degree, compensate for the present deficiency.

Daniel Scovil, Esquire, has forwarded to the Treasurer the sum of £10, by which he wishes to constitute Miss Amy Scovil, of Springfield, a Life Member of the Society.

From the foregoing returns, it appears that the following sums have been contributed to the various objects of the Society for the half year ending at the present time, viz.:— Aged Clergy Fund, £2; Widows' and Orphans' Fund, £6; General Purposes, £1007 2s. 4d., total, £1015 2s. 4d.

The returns from several Local Committees have not yet been received.

From many quarters, it will be observed, that a very large amount has been contributed. This is especially the case with reference to the parishes in Saint John and Portland. From several others, a large proportion of their annual offerings has been forwarded, and from many, the Society might reasonably have expected more.

The present is a time when the Church seems specially called to that Missionary work for which it was instituted. Never, since the first preaching of the Apostles, did there seem a wider field for its extension, than that so remarkably opened up by the extraordinary events of the few past years. The unbeliever alone can fail to see the finger of God in making a way for the soldiers of the Cross to the heathen millions of China, Japan, Africa, and India. This is a subject which might well be brought before all the members of the Society at the Annual Meetings of the several Local Committees. Great benefit would result with increased interest and energy, were the Missionary work of the Church in Great Britain and America, and especially the vast efforts being made at the present time, more generally brought under the notice of the members of the Church.

Pressing wants nearer home may hinder us now from contributing to send forth Missionaries to the heathen; but this subject, duly considered, will hasten the time when at least the spiritual destitution in this Diocese shall be supplied without those means which would otherwise be devoted to teach those "afar off"—who know not God—the way of salvation.

PROCEEDINGS OF THE GENERAL COMMITTEE.

FREDERICTON, JULY 5, 1859.

The Committee met in the Madras School Room at half past six o'clock.

The Right Reverend the Lord Bishop of Fredericton, President &c., in the Chair.

Prayers.

Captain G. Cheyne, R. N., Rev. Philip Wood Loosemore, and J. Robb, M. D., a Select Committee, reported the Lay Delegates duly qualified to represent the Local Committees.

The Clergy present, and the Lay Delegates on this and the succeeding evenings, were the following, with the exception of those marked*, who were not present.

Andover,	Rev. J. S. Hanford,	
Burton,	" A. V. G. Wiggins, D.D.	R. D. Wilmot and G. Clowes.
Canterbury,	" J. Hartin,	Hon. the Attorney General and J. C. Allen.
Carleton,	" F. Coster,	J. Robb, M. D.
Chatham,		Hon. J. A. Street and W. Carman.
Dorchester,		Hon. J. R. Partelow* and J. C. Allen,
Fredericton,		Hon. the Master of the Rolls, and the Hon. Att'y. General.
Gagetown,	" J. Neales,	Hon. the Provincial Secretary, and Hon. J. A. Street.
Glenelg,		Hon. J. S. Saunders and Hon. J. A. Street.
Hampton,		Michean Keator and George Wolhaupter.
Harvey, &c.,		Hon. J. S. Saunders and J. C. Allen.
Kingsclear,	" J. Black,	Geo. Garden and John Lee.
Kingston,		Samuel Foster and Justus Wetmore.*
Lancaster,		Hy. Garbutt* and W. Carman.
Maugerville,	" A. V. G. Wiggins, D.D.	J. D. C. Currie and F. H. Perley.
Portland, St. Paul's,	" C. Lee,	W. Hy. Scovil and H. B. Smith.
Prince William, &c.,	" P. W. Loosemore,	Capt. Cheyne, R. N., and Thos. Jones.
Sackville,		H. B. Allison* and G. Botsford.*
St. Andrews,	" W. Q. Ketchum,	Geo. D. Street* and E. Simonds.
St. George,		Geo. J. Dibblee* and W. H. Scovil.
St. John, St. James,		A. Rainsford Wetmore and H. W. Frith.
St. John, St. Mark's,		T. E. G. Tisdale* and C. H. Fairweather.
St. John, Trinity,		Beverley Robinson* and A. W. Savary.
St. Mary's,	" W. Jaffrey,	J. F. Barker and Chas. Tilley.*
St. Stephen,		N. Marks* and G. S. Grimmer.
Simonds,		John Jordan and R. S. Armstrong.*
Westmorland,		F. A. H. Straton and G. J. Bliss.*
Woodstock,	" S. D. Lee Street,	G. A. Bedell, and W. F. Dibblee.*

W. J. Bedell, Treasurer.

3

The Secretary read Reports of the Missionaries, and the Returns of the Local Committees, and a Report of the proceedings of the Executive Committee. He also read the Report of the Auditors on the Treasurer's Accounts up to the 22d June ultimo.

On motion of Mr. S. Foster—Resolved, That the same be received.

Read by the Lord Bishop, a list of Missions for which appropriations were required.

On motion of the Rev. F. Coster—Resolved, that a Committee be appointed to confer with the Lord Bishop with reference to the Missionary schedule, and also to report to-morrow evening, on the present available funds of the Society, and on the several applications for grants from this Committee. And on motion—Resolved, That the Rev. F. Coster, W. H. Scovil, E. Simonds, and the Secretary, do compose the said Committee.

The Committee adjourned till to-morrow evening at half-past 6 o'clock.

WEDNESDAY EVENING, JULY 6th, 1859.

PRESENT:

The Right Reverend the Lord Bishop &c. &c.

The Clergy and Lay Delegates.

Prayers.

Read Minutes of the last Meeting.

Read by the Secretary some further returns, and a statement of the amount contributed to different objects of the Society. [*See page* 16.]

Rev. F. Coster, from the Committee appointed to confer with the Lord Bishop on the subject of the Missionary Schedule, and to report upon the available funds, presented a report, stating that the Committee had attended to that duty, and recommend that the appropriations for the half year, ending 1st July, 1860, should not exceed £900.

The Schedule was then read over by the Lord Bishop, and each grant having been put separately to the Committee, was carried in the affirmative. Whereupon,

On motion of the Hon. the Provincial Secretary, seconded by the Rev. S. D. Lee Street, it was Resolved unanimously, That the sum of £652 10s. be placed at the disposal of the Lord Bishop for Missionary purposes, agreeably to the following schedule, for the half year ending July 1st, 1860 :—

St. Mary's,	.	.	. £30 0 0	Simonds,	. . .	£37 10 0
Queensbury,	.	.	. 30 0 0	Campobello,	. .	. 25 0 0
				Of which a sum not exceeding £10 per		
Lancaster,	.	.	. 30 0 0	quarter may be allowed for travelling expenses till a Missionary is resident.		
Springfield,	.	.	. 37 10 0	Greenwich,	. .	. 30 0 0
Prince William &c.,	.		. 30 0 0	Buctouche,	. .	. 12 10 0
Curate, St. Stephen,		.	25 0 0	Curate, Woodstock,		. 35 0 0
Douglas, .	.	.	. 45 0 0	Harvey &c.	. .	. 30 0 0
Canterbury,	.	.	. 20 0 0	Moncton.	. .	. 15 0 0
Bathurst,	.	.	. 30 0 0	Blackville.	. .	. 60 0 0
St. David,	.	.	. 30 0 0	Westfield.	. ,	. 30 0 0

At the disposal of the Lord Bishop, £70.

On motion of the Rev. F. Coster, the following grants were unanimously passed :—

To the widow of the late Rev. J. M. Stirling, £12 10s.

To the widow of the late Rev. T. W. Robertson, £12 10s.

To the Treasurer and the Secretary of the Society, each, £12 10s.

To the Executive Committee, for Contingencies, £50.

To the Book Depository Committees of Saint John and Fredericton, for importation of books, £100.

To the Local Committees from the said Depositories, to be appropriated by the Executive Committee, in books, £75.

To aid in building a Church at Salmon River, and at Mechanics' Settlement, County of Albert, each £15, payable when the building is inclosed and the land secured.

To aid in finishing the Church at the Portage, Sussex, £12 10s., payable when the Church is ready for consecration.

Read by the Secretary, applications for aid in repairing the Churches at Mill Town Saint Stephens, and Blackville and Nelson.

Whereupon it was, on motion of the Honorable the Provincial Secretary—Resolved, That whereas the Constitution of the Society precludes the granting aid to the *repairing* of Churches, the above applications cannot be complied with.

On motion of the Rev. Philip W. Loosemore—Resolved, That leave be granted to append to the Annual Report, the statement of the " Clerical Assurance Association" for the past year, the Society not being in any way pledged thereby.

On motion of the Rev. S. D. Lee Street—Resolved, That the Auditor's Report be adopted, and entered upon the Minutes.

On motion of the Rev. F. Coster, the following resolutions were unanimously adopted :—

1. That the Treasurer be requested to close his yearly accounts on the 1st day of May, in each year.

2. That he be requested to transmit his accounts, when made up, to the Auditors, for their audit, and to do so with all practicable dispatch.

3. That the Auditors be requested, as soon as they have completed their audit, to have their report printed, together with all the accounts in detail, under their respective headings of A, B, C, &c.; and

4. That they be requested to lay before the General Committee, at their first meeting, a sufficient number of copies of their report and accounts so printed, as may be required.

5. That this Committee will make provision for the expense so incurred.

It was also, on motion—Resolved, That a blank form of draft on the Treasurer of this Society, by a Missionary, for his salary, be printed and furnished to the Missionaries; such form to bear on the face of it the authority under which the salary is claimed, and the period for which it is claimed.

The Lord Bishop left the chair, and on motion, the Hon. the Provincial Secretary took the same; whereupon it was moved by the Rev. Philip Wood Loosemore, seconded by the Rev. S. D. Lee Street, and resolved unanimously, That the thanks of this Committee be tendered to his Lordship for his able, impartial, and courteous conduct in the chair.

JOHN FREDERICTON, *Chairman.*

WILLIAM Q. KETCHUM, *Secretary.*

AUDITOR'S REPORT.

REPORT " ON THE DIOCESAN CHURCH SOCIETY ACCOUNTS," AS MADE UP BY THE TREASURER, TO 22D JUNE, 1859.

Assets of the 31st December, 1858, per last Audit,			£2,473 0 11

The Treasurer debits himself as follows, as per Account A:

		£	s	d
Sundry Subscriptions,		1,185	17	5
Collections in Churches and Chapels,		26	11	6
Interest collected,		32	10	0

1,244 18 11
£3,717 19 10

Less sundry payments, as per Account B:

	£	s	d
To Missionaries, &c.,	534	3	4
On Grants to Churches and Chapels,	50	0	0
" " to Widows and Orphans,	50	0	0
" " for Books,	100	0	0
Secretary's Salary,	25	0	0
Treasurer's do.	25	0	0
Contingencies,	65	0	6
On Lord Bishop's orders to Missionaries,	30	0	0
" " " for education of children of Clergymen,	6	5	0

885 8 10

Assets of Diocesan Church Society, 22d June, 1859, £2,832 11 0

Which is accounted for as follows:—

	£	s	d
Amount invested per Account C.,	1,584	1	6
Water Debenture, No. 102,	50	0	0
Cash in the Central Bank, and Bank of New Brunswick,	1,198	9	6

2,832 11 0

The FUNDED SECURITIES, as per Treasurer's Account C,

	£	s	d
amounting to	1,584	1	6
Water Debentures, No. 102,	50	0	0

£1634 1 6

Should be divided as follows, viz. :—

"*Seventh Object Fund.*"

	£	s	d
Due this Fund, 31st December, 1858,	446	6	0
130 days interest, to 22d June, 1859,	9	10	7
Special Contribution—(see p. 24 of 23d Report of Diocesan Church Society)—	1	10	0
	£457	6	7
Less granted 19th January, 1859, to the Lord Bishop, to aid in the education of the children of Clergymen,	20	0	0

Due this Fund, 22d June, 1859, £437 6 7

"*Eighth Object Fund.*"

	£	s	d
Due this Fund, 31st December, 1858,	728	12	10
130 days interest, to 22d June, 1859,	15	11	6
Special Contributions—(see p. 24 of 23d Report of Diocesan Church Society)—	9	2	0
	£753	6	4
Granted 19th January, 1859, to Mrs. Stirling and Mrs. Robertson, £25 each,	50	0	0

Carried forward, £803 6 4 £437 6 7 £1634 1 6

Brought forward,		£803	6	4	£437	6	7	£1634	1	6

Less paid to Mrs. Stirling and Mrs. Robertson, grants of 19th January, 1859,   50   0   0

Due this Fund, 22d June, 1859,   .   £753   6   4

"Divinity Scholarship Fund."

Due this Fund, 31st December, 1858,   £94   9   4
130 days interest, to 22d June, 1859,   2   0   2
Special Contribution—(see p. 24 of 23d Report of Diocesan Church Society)—   2   2   6

Due this Fund, 22d June, 1859,   .   £98 12 0

Leaving a balance of the Funded Securities for the credit of the Missionary Fund, or for General Purposes, of 344 16 7

                 £1634   1   6

The CASH BALANCE of £1198   9   6

To the following—viz.:—

"Churches and Chapels."

Due this Fund, 31st December, 1858,   £111 15 7

Less expired grants of 1855, to Churches at Irish Settlement, Springfield, and Portage Church, Sussex, £15 each, and grant of 1856, to Church at Howard Settlement, of £25,   .   55   0   0

         £56 15 7

Granted 19th January, 1859:

Church at Burton,   .   £20   0   0
Do.   at Dalhousie,   .   20   0   0
Do.   at St. Patrick,   .   20   0   0
Do.   at Howard Settlement, 25   0   0
Do.   at Dutch Valley,   .   15   0   0

         100   0   0

         £156 15 7

Less paid in 1859:

Grant of 1858, to Harvey,   £15   0   0
Do.   of 1859, to Burton,   20   0   0
Do.   of 1859, to Dutch Valley, 15   0   0

         50   0   0

Due this Fund, 22d June, 1859,   £106 15 7

The following grants are unpaid:

Grant of 1858, to Hopewell,   £15   0   0
Do.   of 1859, to Dalhousie,   20   0   0
Do.   of 1859, to St. Patrick's, 20   0   0
Do.   of 1859, to Howard Settlement,   .   25   0   0

         £80   0   0

Leaving a balance unappropriated, of   £26 15 7

"Parsonage Houses."

Due this Fund, 31st December, 1858,   £20   0   0
Grant of 1858, to Harvey, unpaid, .   .   .   £20   0   0

Due this Fund, 22d June, 1859,   .   £20   0   0

Carried forward,   .   .   .   £126 15 7   £1198 9 6

Brought forward,	. . .	£126 15 7	£1198 9 6

"*Schools.*"

Due this Fund, 22d June, 1859, same as at last
Audit, ... 3 10 0

"*Grants to the Lord Bishop for the Education
of Sons of Clergymen.*"

Due this Fund, 31st December, 1858, £43 15 0
Granted 19th January, 1859, . . 20 0 0

£63 15 0
Less paid in 1859, . . . 6 5 0

Due this Fund, 22d June, 1859, . £57 10 0—£187 15 7

Granted 19th Jan'y. 1859, for sundry Missions, £1,105 0 0

Am't. of Grants.	Parish or Missions.	Am't. Paid.*
£60 0 0	St. Mary's,	£15 0 0
30 0 0	Simonds,	7 10 0
60 0 0	Queensbury,	15 0 0
50 0 0	Campobello,	0 0 0
80 0 0	Lancaster,	20 0 0
60 0 0	Springfield,	15 0 0
60 0 0	Greenwich,	20 0 0
60 0 0	Prince William,	15 0 0
60 0 0	Welford,	15 0 0
25 0 0	Buctouche,	6 5 0
50 0 0	Curate of St. Stephen,	12 10 0
50 0 0	Do. of Woodstock,	12 10 0
60 0 0	Douglas,	15 0 0
60 0 0	Harvey,	15 0 0
30 0 0	Howard Settlement,	0 0 0
30 0 0	Moncton,	7 10 0
40 0 0	Bathurst,	10 0 0
120 0 0	Blackville & Nelson,	30 0 0
60 0 0	Canning,	15 0 0
60 0 0	St. David's,	0 0 0

£246 5 0

£1105 0 0

Due on this grant, 22d June, 1859, . £858 15 0

* These payments are for salaries to the several Missionaries, for
quarter ending 31st March, 1859, excepting Lancaster and Greenwich, which are special payments, on the Lord Bishop's orders.

Granted 19th January, 1859, for Missionary purposes, at the Lord Bishop's disposal, . £90 0 0
Less paid in 1859, on order to W. Q. Ketchum,
as Missionary to Maryland, . £20 0 0
On Rev. W. H. Street's order, Missionary
at Canning. *The Treasurer certifies, on
the voucher No.* 41, *that it was paid by
the Lord Bishop's directions,* . 10 0 0
30 0 0

Due on this grant, 22d June, 1859, . £60 0 0

From the Cash Balance, 22d June, 1859, of Treasurer's
Accounts, of £1198 9 6
Must be deducted—
Due to Churches and Chapels, per sheet No. 3, 106 15 7
Do. Parsonage Houses, do. 20 0 0

Carried forward, . . £126 15 7 £1198 9 6

Brought forward, . .	£126 15 7	£1198 9 6
Due to Schools, per sheet No. 3,	3 10 0	
Do. on grant for the education of the Sons		
of Clergymen, per sheet No. 3, .	57 10 0	
On grants to Missions, sheet No. 4, .	858 15 0	
On grants, for Missionaries, at the disposal of the		
Lord Bishop, sheet No. 4, . .	60 0 0	
		£1106 10 7

Leaving a cash balance, 22d June, 1859, of .   .   £91 18 11
   At the disposal of the Society,

Vouchers accompanied the Treasurer's Accounts, and are in order, excepting No. 41, already noticed, and Nos. 3 and 4, which are dated January, 1858, should be 1859.

Respectfully submitted.

WM. HY. SCOVIL, Auditor.

St. John, N. B., July 4, 1859.

Fredericton, 6th July, 1859.

The Fredericton Book Depository Committee show the following statement:—

Balance of Stock, 30th June, 1859, .	.£247 1 9
Do. of Cash do. .	. 18 1 9
	£265 3 6

WM. HY. SCOVIL.

ANNIVERSARY MEETING.

The Anniversary Meeting was held in the Madras School
Room, at 7 o'clock.

PRESENT:

His Excellency the Honorable J. H. T. Manners Sutton,
Lieut. Governor, &c., &c., &c., Patron, in the Chair.
The Right Reverend the Lord Bishop of Fredericton,
President.
The Honorable Mr. Justice Neville Parker, V. P.
The Honorable the Provincial Secretary, V. P.
The Clergy and Lay Delegates, and a large assembly of
other members of the Society.

PRAYERS.

His Excellency addressed the meeting, and called upon
the Secretary to read the Report.

Whereupon, it was moved by the Right Reverend the
Lord Bishop, seconded by J. Robb, Esq., M. D., and Resolved unanimously, That the Report be adopted, and
printed under the direction of the Executive Committee.

Moved by A. W. Savary, Esq., seconded by the Rev. S.
D. Lee Street, and Resolved unanimously, That the success
vouchsafed to the Society, at this its first Anniversary Meeting under the change in the Constitution, encourages the
hope, that, by the blessing of God, its sphere of usefulness
may thereby be increased.

Moved by the Honorable the Provincial Secretary,
seconded by the Rev. Philip Wood Loosemore, and Resolved unanimously, That whereas the missionary work of
the Church is of such vast interest and importance, the
Society would recommend that this subject be brought
more generally before its members at the Annual Meetings
of the Local Committees, both with regard to the spiritual
destitution in this Diocese, and also with reference to Missions in heathen countries.

Moved by the Honorable the Attorney General, seconded
by W. Carman, Esq., and Resolved unanimously, That the
best thanks of this meeting be offered to the Officers of the
Society for their efficient services during the past year; and
further Resolved, That the following Gentlemen be the
Officers of the Society for the ensuing year:—

William J. Bedell, Esq., *Treasurer.*
Rev. William Q. Ketchum, M. A., *Secretary.*
W. Henry Scovil, Esq., } *Auditors.*
C. H. Fairweather, Esq., }

4

And further Resolved, that the Executive Committee, elected at the last Anniversary Meeting, do continue in office till the first Thursday in July next.

His Excellency was pleased to leave the Chair, and on motion, the Lord Bishop took the same:

Whereupon, it was moved by the Honorable Mr. Justice Neville Parker, seconded by the Rev. Charles Lee, and Resolved unanimously, That the thanks of the Society be respectfully tendered to His Excellency for his presence and support on the present occasion, and for his kind and courteous conduct in the Chair.

J. H. T. MANERS SUTTON, Chairman.

William Q. Ketchum, Secretary.

REPORT OF THE PROCEEDINGS OF THE EXECUTIVE COMMITTEE FOR THE PAST HALF YEAR.

The Minutes of the meetings held in January and March last, will be found published in the 23rd Report, (p. 38–42).

The Committee met at St. John. on the 1st of June.

An abstract of the Treasurer's Account to date, was read, and ordered to be filed.

The following accounts were read, and ordered to be paid:

Barnes & Co., for printing the 23rd Report, £49 9s. 6d.

The Secretary, for postage and travelling expenses, £3 7s. 8d.

A select Committee was appointed to make arrangements for the Anniversary Meeting at Fredericton.

The Committee met at Fredericton July 8th, the day after the Anniversary Meeting of the Society, when the following accounts were read, and ordered to be paid:—

Expenses incurred at the late meetings, £2 5s.

The Secretary, for travelling and contingent expenses, postages, &c., £4 17s. 6d.

It was, on motion, Resolved, That 3000 copies of the Report be printed, and that Mr. R. F. Hazen, Mr. C. H. Fairweather, Mr. H. W. Frith, and the Secretary, do attend to that duty, and that they require tenders for the work.

It was Resolved, That the Book Depository Committees of St. John and Fredericton be continued for the ensuing year; and also, That the Loan Committee be continued for the ensuing year; and further Resolved,

That the Loan Committee be requested, by communication with the Treasurer, to ascertain the amount of funds which may not be required to meet the appropriations made by the General Committee, and to invest, or place the same at interest, in such a manner that the amount can be called for at the next Annual Meeting of the Society.

Resolved, That the Books granted by the General Committee, to the amount of £75, be distributed in accordance with the scale adopted in March last, and printed in the Report—Moncton being substituted for Victoria—the rate to be 50 per cent.

TREASURER'S ACCOUNTS.

[A]

The Diocesan Church Society in Account with W. J. BEDELL, *Treasurer.*

1859.   SUBSCRIPTIONS AND DONATIONS RECEIVED.

			£	s	d
Jan. Rec'd. from Rev. Dr. Wiggins,	Maugerville, &c.,		17	18	2
" " C. Milner,	Westfield,		13	10	4
" " Dr. G. J. Jarvis,	Shediac,		8	10	0
" " T. Hartin,	Canterbury,		8	7	9
" R. DeVeber, Esq.,	St. John.		101	18	5
" Rev. W. Cruden	Nelson, &c.			12	6
" G. Ingraham, Esq.	Queensbury,		5	12	2
" C. W. Wardlaw, Esq.	St. Andrews,		34	1	7
" Rev. W. Q. Ketchum,	Grand Manan,		5	0	0
" " William Jaffrey,	St. Mary's		14	0	0
" " S. Bacon,	Chatham,		20	7	6
" " P. W. Loosemore,	Prince William,		24	3	1
" " H. B. Nichols,	Hopewell, &c.,		7	10	0
" " C. Lee,	St. Pauls,		27	10	7
" " D. J. Wetmore,	Weldford,		3	7	6
" " J. Hudson,	Miramichi,		4	11	2
" " J. S. Thomson,	St. David,		13	0	0
" Mrs. Gordon,	Bathurst,			10	0
" Rev. J. McGivern,	St. George,		17	10	0
" " J. Black,	Kingsclear,		18	13	3½
" " A. Wood,	Cambridge,		3	16	3
" " J. S. Hanford,	Andover,		20	6	4
" " G. G. Roberts,	Douglas,		17	11	3
" " W. Q. Ketchum,	add. Kingston,			12	2
" " do.	(H. T. Gilbert,) St. John,		1	0	0
" " do.	(Dr. Bayard,) Nerepis,		1	0	0
" " do.	Campobello,		1	7	6
" " do.	Gagetown,		1	10	0
" " do.	Portland,		20	0	0
" " G. C. Wiggins,	Petersville,		10	11	1
" J. B. Whipple, Esq.,	Victoria,		5	5	0
" Rev. J. S. Williams,	Campobello,		11	0	0
" " G. Bedell,	Lancaster,		28	5	6
" " Mr. Harrison,	Portland,		14	12	0
Feb'y " " Mr. Ketchum,	Richibucto,		6	17	0
" J. A. Street, Esq.,	Bathurst,		5	15	9
" Hon. E. B. Chandler,	(Mr. DeWolf,) Sackville,		25	16	0
" Rev. Mr. Warneford,			12	7	5
" C. Dixon, Esq.,	Norton,		8	8	0
" Rev. W. H. DeVeber,			30	15	6
March " Mr. Desbrisay,	(Rev. A. N. Coster,) Richibucto,		1	10	9½
" Rev. S. D. L. Street,	Woodstock,		35	1	1½
" " W. Q. Ketchum,	Westmorland,		10	5	4½
April " " H. B. Nichols,	Hopewell,		11	15	10
" " G. G. Roberts,	Douglas,		7	10	0
" W. B. Scovil, Esq.,	Springfield,		1	14	0
" Rev. C. F. Street,	Bathurst,		7	10	0
" " W. Q. Ketchum,	Fredericton & Maryland,		143	2	0
" " Mr. Walker,	(per Son,)			10	3

Carried forward, ... £792 10 2

1859.	Brought forward,	. . . . .	£792 10 2
June. Rec'd. from S. D. L. Street,	Wooodstock,		26 0 0
" W. E. Scovil,	Kingston,		15 0 0

Deposited in Bank of New Brunswick, by

Rev. F. Coster,	Carleton,	21 11 3
H. W. Frith, Esq.	St. John,	80 0 0
Rev. H. Pollard,	St. Stephen,	14 19 3
The Lord Bishop	(from a Churchman),	2 0 0
L. H. DeVeber, Esq.,	Gagetown,	15 0 0
Rev. J. W. Disbrow,	Simonds,	13 12 6
Rev. W. H. Street,	Canning,	5 17 10
Mr. Walker,		28 4 7
Rev. T. McGhee,	Sussex,	10 16 0
H. W. Frith,	St. John,	8 5 0
J. V. Thurgar, Esq.,	St. John,	152 0 0
		£1,185 17 5

Collections.

Rec'd. from J. V. Thurgar, Esq., Trinity, St. John,	£19 17 6
" Rev. W. E. Scovil, Kingston,	5 0 0
" " A. Wood, Cambridge,	1 14 0
	£26 11 6

Interest.

May. Rec'd. from M. Mackey, on C. P. Wetmore's mortgage,	£3 0 0
" J. Dibblee, on his mortgage,	4 10 0
" A. Arnold, do.	6 0 0
" J. F. W. Winslow, do.	6 0 0
" E. W. Miller, do.	10 0 0
" William McKeen, do.	3 0 0
	£32 10 0

RECAPITULATED.

Contributions,	- - - -	£1,185 17 5
Collections in Churches, -	. . .	26 11 6
Interest on Mortgages,	. . .	32 10 0
E. & O. E.		£1,244 18 11

W. J. BEDELL, Treasurer.

Fredericton, June 22, 1859.

[B]

The Diocesan Church Society, in Account with Wm. J. Bedell, *Treasurer.*

1859.	Vouchers. No.				£ s d
Jan. 3.	1.	Paid Rev. G. G. Roberts,	Douglas,		£15 0 0
	2.	" W. H. Street,	Canning,		25 0 0
	3.	" W. N. Boyer,	Moncton,		7 10 0
	4.	" T. Hartin,	Canterbury,		15 0 0
	5.	" H. Pollard,	St. Stephen,		41 13 4
	6.	" G. Bedell,	Lancaster,		20 0 0
		Carried forward,	. . . .		£124 3 4

		Brought forward, ...		£124	3	4

1859.	Vouchers. No.						
Jan.	9.	"	A. H. Weeks,	Buctouche,	6	5	0
	10.	"	G. C. Wiggins,	Petersville,	15	0	0
	11.	"	J. W. Disbrow,	Simonds,	7	10	0
	12.	"	D. J. Wetmore,	Weldford,	15	0	0
	13.	"	W. Jaffrey,	St. Mary's,	15	0	0
	14.	"	H. B. Nichols,	Hopewell,	15	0	0
	16.	"	P. W. Loosemore,	Prince William,	15	0	0
	17.	"	H. W. Tippett,	Queensbury,	15	0	0
	18.	"	J. S. Thomson,	St. David,	15	0	0
Feb. 9.	25.	"	J. S. Williams,	Campobello,	12	10	0
	27.	"	W. Cruden,	Nelson, &c.	25	0	0
Apr. 1.	29.	"	P. W. Loosemore,	Prince William,	15	0	0
	30.	"	C. P. Bliss,	Springfield,	15	0	0
	31.	"	D. J. Wetmore,	Weldford,	15	0	0
	32.	"	W. Jaffrey,	St. Mary's,	15	0	0
	33.	"	E. S. Woodman,	Woodstock,	12	10	0
	34.	"	W. Cruden,	Nelson, &c.,	30	0	0
	36.	"	W. N. Boyer,	Moncton,	7	10	0
	37.	"	A. H. Weeks,	Buctouche,	6	5	0
	38.	"	J. W. Disbrow,	Simonds,	7	10	0
	39.	"	C. F. Street,	Bathurst,	7	10	0
	40.	"	W. H. Street,	Canning,	15	0	0
	42.	"	H. B. Nichols,	Hopewell,	15	0	0
	43.	"	G. G. Roberts,	Douglas,	15	0	0
	44.	"	C. F. Street,	Bathurst,	10	0	0
	45.	"	The Lord Bishop's order to Mr. Garbutt,	Lancaster,	20	0	0
May.	46.	"	Rev. W. H. Tippett,	Queensbury,	15	0	0
	47.	"	H. Pollard,	St. Stephen,	12	10	0
	50.	"	Order, bal. due Rev. G. C. Wiggins,	Petersville,	5	0	0
	48.		Lord Bishop's order, Rev. J. Neales, for Missionary services at Petersville,		15	0	0

	£534	3	4

Churches and Chapels.

Jan'y. 15.	Paid Rev. H. B. Nichols, Church at Harvey,		.	£15	0	0
March 28.	" N. Hubbard, Esq., " Burton,		.	20	0	0
April. 35.	" Rev. T. McGhee, " Dutch Valley,		.	15	0	0

	£50	0	0

Widows and Orphans.

Feb'y. 24.	Paid Mrs. E. Robertson's order, .	.	£25	0	0
	26. " Mrs. R. S. Stirling's " .	.	25	0	0

	£50	0	0

The Lord Bishop's Orders.

Feb'y. 23.	Paid order to Rev. W. Q. Ketchum, for Missionary services for the past year, for Maryland,	. £20	0	0
April. 41.	Paid Rev. W. H. Street's order on Lord Bishop, for Canning, . . .	. 10	0	0

	£30	0	0

1859. Vouchers. No.   *Education.*

Feb'y. 49. Paid the Lord Bishop's order to Rev. W. H. Tippett,   £6   5   0

Book Committee.
21. Paid Book Committee's order, .   .   .£100   0   0

Jan'y. 19. Paid Secretary's salary,   .   .   .£25   0   0
      "   Treasurer's   "   .   .   . 25   0   0

                                       £50   0   0

Contingencies.

Jan'y. 7. Paid Ward C. Drury, Registrar, for DeWolf Estate, £0 14   0
     8.   "   the Secretary, Postage and Stationery,   .   1 11   5
    20.   "   Rev. Mr. Ketchum, for J. Whitney, per bill, Expenses of Annual Meeting at St. John,   .   4   3   2
    22.   "   Secretary's expenses, attending Meeting, &c.   .   4   9   9
June. 52.   "   Order to Barnes & Co., Printing Reports,   . 49   9   6
    53.   "   Secretary's expenses, per bill,   .   3   7   8
       "   Treasurer, for Postage and Stationery,   .   1   5   0

                                       £65   0   6

RECAPITULATED.

Missionary Visits,	.£534 8 4
Churches and Chapels,	50 0 0
Widows and Orphans, .	. 50 0 0
Lord Bishop's Orders,	30 0 0
Education, .	6 5 0
Book Committee,	100 0 0
Secretary and Treasurer,	50 0 0
Contingencies,	65 0 6

                                       £885   8 10

              E. & O. E.   W. J. BEDELL, Treasurer.
Fredericton, June 22, 1859.

[C]

Amount of Loans from the Funds of the Diocesan Church Society, with Interest received in 1859.

When Loaned.	To Whom.	Date to which Interest has been paid.	Amounts Loaned.			Interest received.		
Sept. 5, 1848.	Amos Arnold.	Sept. 5, 1858.	£100	0	0	£6	0	0
" 15, "	A. M'Lean.	" 15, "	209	1	6			
" 16, "	J. F. W. Winslow.	" 16, "	100	0	0	6	0	0
" 17, 1852.	Wm. M'Keen.	Mar. 17, "	100	0	0	3	0	0
" 8, 1850.	J. Dibblee.	" 8, 1859.	150	0	0	4	10	0
Feb. 14, 1852.	C. P. Wetmore.	May 14, "	100	0	0	3	0	0
Oct. 15, "	E. W. Miller.	Feb. 7, 1856.	170	0	0	10	0	0
" 16, "	J. A. Maclauchlin.	Oct. 16, 1858.	250	0	0			
Feb. 2, 1854.	W. Lawrence.	May 2, "	130	0	0			
May 2, "	W. Plant.	Nothing paid.	75	0	0			
Oct. 19, 1855.	Water Company.		200	0	0			
	E. & O. E.		£1584	1	6	£32	10	0

Fredericton, June 25, 1859.   W. J. BEDELL, Treasurer.

[D]

Statement of Funds of the Diocesan Church Society.

Balance per last Audit,	.	.	.	.	£838 19 5
Contributions per Account A.,	.	.	.	.	1,185 17 5
Collections in Churches,	.	.	.	.	26 11 6
Interest received since last Audit,	.	.	.	.	32 10 0

	£2,083 18 4
Paid per Account B., ...	885 8 10

	£1,198 9 6

In Central Bank, . . .	. £288 16 11	
In Bank of New Brunswick, . .	. 909 12 11	
		£1,198 9 10

E. & O. E.   W. J. BEDELL, TREASURER.

Fredericton, June 22, 1859.

Abstract Account of the Fredericton Book Depository Committee of the Diocesan Church Society, from 31st Dec. 1858, to 30th June, 1859.

1858.			
Dec. 31.	Books on hand this date, . .		£189 3 0
	Books received from the Society for Promoting		
	Christian Knowledge, . .		78 18 0
			£268 1 0

1859.	CONTRA.		
June 30.	Books sold during the half year,	. £20 19 3	
	Balance of Stock. . .	. 247 1 9	
			£268 1 0

1859.	CASH ACCOUNT.		
Jan. 1.	Balance on hand this date, . .		£45 5 9
June. 30.	Sales during the half year. .		20 19 3
	Grant to the Fredericton Depository, .		50 0 0
			£116 5 0

1859.	CONTRA.		
Feb. 16.	Paid for Bill of Exchange, £54 14s. 4d.		
	sterling—Currency, .	. £66 17 6	
	". M'Millan's acc't. for Hymn-books,	12 10 6	
	" W. Wright, Esquire, Saint John		
	Depository, .	. 16 17 6	
	" Commission, &c. to Depositor,	; 1 17 9	
June 30.	Cash balance on hand this date,	. 18 1 9	
			£116 5 0

	SUMMARY.		
	Balance of Cash, . .	. £18 1 9	
	Do. of Stock, . .	. 247 1 9	
		£265 3 6	

Examined and approved at a meeting of the Fredericton Depository Committee, 3d July, 1859.

W. Q. KETCHUM, SECRETARY.

SCHEDULE OF APPROPRIATIONS

CHURCH SOCIETY OF NEW BRUNSWICK.

1838 to 1853. See 17th Report, page 38–42, £9,988 15 6
1853 to 1856. See 20th Report, page 44,   13,891 4 1
1857.   See 21st Report, page 45,   1,400 0 0
1858.   See 22d Report, page 50,   1,600 0 0
1859.   See 23d Report, page 50,   1,550 0 0
July, 1859. Missionary purposes, £652 10 0
            Widows' Pensions,   25 0 0
            Churches,   .   .   42 10 0
            Books,   .   . 100 0 0
            Officers of Society, . 25 0 0
            Contingencies,   .   50 0 0
                                 —————   895 0 0
                                        ————————————
                                        £29,324 19 7

LIST OF CONTRIBUTORS

TO THE DIOCESAN CHURCH SOCIETY OF NEW BRUNSWICK.

Life Members.

By the payment of not less than Ten Pounds at any one time.—Those
marked with A. S., are also Annual Subscribers.

1838. BAILLIE, Hon. THOMAS.
MACLAUCHLAN, JAMES A. Esquire, A. S.
WETMORE, JUSTUS S. Esquire, A. S.

1839. BOTSFORD, Hon. WILLIAM, V. P., A. S.
ROBINSON, Hon. F. P., A. S.
SCOVIL, Rev. WILLIAM, A. S.

1840. PARKER, Hon. NEVILLE, Master of the Rolls, V. P., A. S.
ROBINSON, Colonel JOHN, V. P. A. S.

1842. RATCHFORD, E. D. W. Esquire.

1843. SMITH, HENRY BOWYER, Esquire, V. P., A. S.

1845. COLEBROOKE, His Excellency Sir WILLIAM, M. G., C. B. K. H.,
late Lieutenant-Governor and Commander in-Chief.

1846. FREDERICTON, The Right Reverend JOHN, Lord Bishop of,
President, A. S.
GILBERT, GEORGE G. Esquire.
PARKER, Hon. Mr. Justice, A. S.
SAUNDERS, Hon. JOHN S. V. P.
SMITH, G. SIDNEY, A. S.
TILLEY, Hon. S. L., V. P. A. S.
WIGGINS, STEPHEN, Esquire, A. S.
WIGGINS, FREDERICK A. Esquire, V. P., A. S.

1847. READE, ALFRED, Esquire.
SEARS, EDWARD, Esquire, A. S.
WIGGINS, Mrs. STEPHEN, A. S.

1848. HENDERSON, EDMOND, Captain R. E.

1849. HEAD, His Excellency Sir EDMUND WALKER, Baronet, late
Lieutenant-Governor and Commander-in-Chief, &c. &c.

1850. FAIRWEATHER, JOSEPH, Esquire, A. S.
DESBRISAY, L. P. W., Esquire, A. S.

1851. SCOVIL, DANIEL, Esquire, A. S.
SCOVIL, W. HENRY, Esquire, A. S.

1852. SMITH, HENRY BOWYER, Junior, A. S.
SCOVIL, EDWARD G., A. S.

1853. SCOVIL, Mrs. W. H., A. S.

1854. MANNERS SUTTON, His Excellency The Honorable J. H. T., Lieut.
Governor and Commander-in-Chief, &c. &c., Patron, A. S.
SCOVIL, A. ISABEL, A. S.
NEALES, Rev. JAMES, A. S.

1855. SIMONDS, Mrs. RICHARD, Senior, A. S.

1856. THOMSON, Miss ANNE.
SCOVIL, Miss AMELIA B., A. S.
BEDELL, Rev. G., A. S.

1857. HANINGTON, DANIEL J., A. S.
WRIGHT, WILLIAM, Esquire, D. C. L. A. S.

1858. HALL, Mr. S. S., A. S.
FAIRWEATHER, C. H., A. S.
SCOVIL, S. JOHN.
SHORTLAND, Captain, R. N.

1859. SCOVIL, Miss AMY.

SUBSCRIPTIONS FOR 1859.

ANDOVER AND GRAND FALLS.

Name	£	s	d
Armstrong, Mrs.	£0	1	3
Armstrong, David J.		1	3
Baird, Mrs.		1	3
Baird, Mrs. H.		2	6
Baird, Mr. and Mrs. Adam		5	0
Baird, Mr. and Mrs. Geo.		5	0
Baird, Margaret		1	3
Beardsley, Mrs. Paul		5	0
Beckwith, Sheriff		10	0
Beckwith, Miss		5	0
Bedell, Mrs.		10	0
Bedell, Jane H.		5	0
Bedell, William C.		1	3
Bedell, Thomas P.		1	3
Bedell, Elizabeth E.		1	3
Bedell, Agnes		1	3
Bull, Charles A.		2	6
Cox, George		5	0
Curry, George W.	1	0	0
Curry, Mr. and Mrs. Wm.		5	0
Hammond, Mrs. C. A.		10	0
Harper, Aaron		5	0
Hartt, N. Beckwith		5	0
Miller, Andrew Jun.		2	6
Miller, Mr. and Mrs. Wm.		5	0
Miller, William Jun.		1	3
Miller, Emmeline		1	3
Miller, Mr. and Mrs. John		5	0
Missionary S. P. G.	2	0	0
Newcomb, William R.		7	6
Pickett, Lewis	1	0	0
Pickett, Mrs. D.		5	0
Pickett, John		5	0
Rainsford, A. W.	1	0	0
Rainsford, Osmond		5	0
Raymond, Mr. and Mrs.		7	6
Reed, Mr. and Mrs.		10	0
Ritchey, William		1	3
Sawyer, James,		1	3
Scott, William		5	0
Watson, Mr. and Mrs. Wm.		7	6
Watson, Mr. and Mrs. Sam.		10	0
Watson, William Jun.		2	6
Watson, Sarah		2	6
West, Miss		2	6
1st Sermon,	3	1	6
	£16	19	0

BATHURST, SALMON BEACH, &c.
BATHURST.

Name	£	s	d
Baldwin, H. W.	£0	10	0
Bishop, Dr.		10	0
Bateman, Mrs.		1	3
Carman, Mrs.		5	0
Carter, J. T.		5	0
Cole, Mrs.		2	6

Name	£	s	d
DesBrisay, Theophilus	£0	10	0
Doran, J. R.		5	0
Ellis, R.		5	0
Ellis, R. and T.		5	0
End, Mrs.		15	0
Friend,		12	6
Friend,		10	0
Florence, Miss		5	0
Harrison, Mrs.		1	3
Hinton, Mrs.		5	0
Hinton, Miss S.		1	3
Hinton, M.		1	3
Morrow, Mr.		5	0
O'Brien, John		5	0
Proctor, Mrs.		2	6
Paul, J. W.		2	6
Raltt, Mrs.		2	6
Read, Mrs.		12	6
Read, Miss		5	0
Read, Sarah H.		5	0
Read, Mary and Emma		5	0
Smith, G. & A.	1	0	0
Sutherland, Mary		1	3
Sutherland, G.		1	3
Sutherland, C.		1	3
Sutherland, George		1	3
Street, Rev. C. F.	1	5	0
Wilson, George	1	0	0
	£11	5	0

SALMON BEACH.

Name	£	s	d
Glendinning, J. Jun.	£0	1	3
Glendinning, E. J.			7½
Glendinning, Margaret		1	3
Goode, Peter		2	6
Miller, Richard		5	0
Smith, Henry B.		2	6
Smith, Thomas		1	3
Smith, John		1	3
Smith, Matthew			7½
Smith, Elizabeth			7½
Smith, Mrs. J.		5	0
	£1	1	10½

NEW BANDON.

Name	£	s	d
Chamberlain, Isaac	£0	1	3
Dempsey, John		1	3
Eddy, Ann		1	3
Forbes, Mary Ann		2	6
Forbes, Rachel		1	3
Forbes, William		1	3
Friend,		5	0
Good, Nicholas		1	3
Hillock, Thomas		1	0
Hillock, John		1	0
Hillock, Jane		1	1½
Jagoe, Walter		1	3
Jeffers, M. J.		1	3

	£	s	d
Knowles, Mrs. T.	£0	2	0
Knowles, Mary Ann			10
Knowles, H. Jane			4½
Parrott, Matthew		1	3
Smith, John B.		1	8
Collection at Dalhousie,	1	0	0
Do. Flat Lands,		5	0
Do. Caraquet,	3	3	1½
	£5	14	5½

BLACKVILLE AND NELSON.

BLACKVILLE.

	£	s	d
Astle, David	£0	2	6
Conners, Charles		5	0
Conners, William		5	0
Coughlin, Benjamin		5	0
Coughlin, Elizabeth		8	0
Coughlin, John Tryan		2	6
Coughlin, William		2	6
Coughlin, David		2	6
Curtis, David		5	0
Curtis, Joseph Henry		8	0
Curtis, William Applan		2	6
Curtis, Thomas O.		2	6
Friend, A		2	6
Gillespie, James		1	3
Gillespie, Theophilus		2	6
Hambrook, Mrs.		2	6
Hambrook, Mark		2	6
Harris, Moses		2	6
M'Arthur, Robert		5	0
M'Kennon, Mrs.		1	3
Morrison, John		2	6
Nutbeam, James		2	6
Scofield, Richard		3	1½
Smith, James		2	6
Vanderbeck, Alexander		2	6
Offerings after Churchings,		3	3½
Collection,		2	8
	£4	8	6

NELSON.

	£	s	d
Allison, Mrs.	£0	2	6
Allison, William		2	6
Ambrose, Thomas		8	9
Astle, Leonard		2	6
Astle, Ann Elizabeth		1	3
Astle, Mrs. John		1	3
Astle, Matilda			7½
Astle, Mrs. James		1	3
Bateman, Frances Jane		1	3
Bateman, William		1	0
Bateman, Richard		1	0
Bateman, Joseph		1	0
Betts, Mrs.		2	6
Carmault, Mrs.		1	3
Carmault, James		1	3
Cliff, George		3	9
Cliff, William		3	1½
Crocker, Mrs. William G.		1	3
Cruden, William M.	1	0	0

	£	s	d
Cruden, Mrs.	£0	10	0
Cruden, Rev. William	1	0	0
Davidson, Robert		5	0
Davidson, Abbot		5	0
Davidson, Alexander		5	0
Davidson, James Ledden		1	3
Friend, A		5	0
Friend, A			11
Graham, Thomas		1	3
Hartt, Daniel		5	0
Hosford, Benjamin		1	3
Hosford, William		1	3
Leighton, Mrs.		1	3
M'Ghee, Mrs.		5	0
M'Kenzie, Mrs.		2	6
M'Kenzie, William		2	6
Mewes, Robert		2	6
Newman, David James		1	3
Newman, John		2	6
Poke, William		1	6
Poke, Mrs.		1	3
Poke, Elizabeth		1	0
Poke, Alexander			7½
Saunders, Alexander		5	0
Saunders, Mrs.		2	6
Saunders, Josephine		1	3
Saunders, Eliza		1	3
Vye, Mrs. Henry		1	3
Vye, James		2	6
Vye, Joseph		1	3
Weston, Mrs.		1	3
Weston, Matilda		1	3
Weston, Joseph Jun.		1	6
Williston, Edward		5	0
Collections,		12	7½
	£8	12	5

CANNING AND CHIPMAN.

	£	s	d
Burpee, E.	£0	5	0
Burpee, J.		5	0
Earle, Honorable John		10	0
Goldfinch, J. W.		5	0
M'Dougal, Mrs.		1	3
Street, Rev. W. H.		10	0
Thorne, Stephen		3	1½
Yeamans, Richard,		10	0
Yeamans, Robert		5	0
	£2	14	4½

CAMPOBELLO.

	£	s	d
A little girl,	£0	1	6
Batson, John		1	10½
Beatty, Mrs.		1	3
Brown, Major		2	6
Byron, Luke		2	6
Calder, James		2	6
Chapman, Richard			7½
Flagg, Price		2	6
Flagg, Arthur		1	3
Flagg, Mrs. D.		2	6

	£	s	d			£	s	d
Flagg, Joanna	£0	1	3	Hamilton, James	£0	1	3
Gilligan, William		1	3	Hamilton, Mrs. James		1	3
Gregg, John		2	6	Heatherington, John		1	3
Kendrick, Nancy		8	1½	Heatherington, Mrs.		1	3
Lank, Mary		1	3	Heatherington, John Jun.		1	3
Moses, Captain		5	0	Heatherington, Elizabeth		1	3
Moses, Mrs.		5	0	Jarvis, John		1	3
Moses, Miss		1	10½	Muxou, John		1	3
Mitchell, Hibbert			7½	Murun, Mrs. John		1	3
Pitts, Mrs.		1	3	Mackay, William		1	3
Price, Isaac		3	1½	Maubray, Thomas		1	3
Robinson, Captain R. N.	1	0	0	Maubray, Mrs.		1	3
Robinson, Mrs.	1	0	0	Maubray, Everene		1	3
Robinson, Miss		10	0	Mattatoll, Levi		1	3
Shasland, Mrs.		1	3	Mattatoll, Mrs.		1	3
Sumner, Mrs.		2	3	Mattatoll, William			7½
Swim, Mrs.		1	3	Miller, David			7½
Vennell, John		1	3	Miller, Mrs. David			7½
Williams, John		2	6	M'Mullan, James			7½
Collection in June,	2	2	6	M'Mullan, Mrs.			7½
	£7	7	0	M'Mullan, George		1	3
				M'Mullan, Andrew			7½
CANTERBURY.				M'Mullan, Ann			7½
Anderson, Robert	£0	0	7½	M'Illroy, John Sen.		1	3
Anderson, Mrs. Robert			7½	M'Illroy, Mrs. John		1	3
Blair, John Jun.		2	6	M'Illroy, Allen		1	3
Blair, Mrs. John		2	6	M'Illroy, Mrs. Allen		1	3
Boyd, Catherine			7½	M'Illroy, Archibald		1	3
Cunningham, Thos. Sen.		1	3	M'Illroy, Mrs. Archibald		1	3
Cunningham, Mrs. Thos.		1	3	M'Illroy, Jero		1	3
Cunningham, Thomas Jun.		5	0	M'Illroy, Mrs. Jero		1	3
Cunningham, William Sen.		1	3	M'Illroy, Ward		1	3
Cunningham, Margaret		1	3	M'Illroy, Mrs. Ward		1	3
Cunningham, Andrew		1	3	M'Illroy, William			7½
Cunningham, Thomas		1	3	M'Kinney, Joseph		1	3
Cunningham, William Jun.		1	3	M'Kinney, James		1	3
Cunningham, Mrs. Wm.		1	3	M'Kinney, Mrs.		1	3
Cunningham, James		1	3	M'Kay, Hugh.		2	6
Cunningham, Mrs. James		1	3	M'Kay, Mrs.		1	3
Cripps, Mrs.		1	3	M'Kay, Hughina		1	6
Dougherty, George		1	3	M'Kay, Joan		1	3
Dougherty, Mrs.			7½	Quigley, Mary Ann		1	3
Dow, John (Grass Lake),		1	3	Robinson, James		1	3
English, James		1	3	Robinson, Mrs. James		1	3
English, Mrs. James		1	3	Robinson, George Sen.		2	6
Grosvenor, S. G.		5	0	Robinson, Mrs. George		2	6
Garden, Edward		1	3	Tripp, William		2	6
Graham, George		1	3	Tripp, Mrs. William		1	3
Graham, Mrs. George		1	3	Tripp, Anne E.			7½
Graham, James		1	3	Winters, Nathaniel		1	3
Graham, Edward		1	3	Winters, Charles		1	3
Graham, William Jun.		1	3	Winters, Mrs. Charles		1	3
Graham, Mrs.		1	3	Worth, Godfrey		1	3
Hartin, Rev. Thomas		10	0	Worth, Mrs.		1	3
Hartin, Mrs.		10	0	Walling, William		1	3
Hartin, John Medley		5	0	Walling, Mrs.		1	3
Hartin, Marcus		1	3	Walling, Hugh			7½
Hartin, Mrs. Marcus			7½	Wilson, Mrs.			7½
Hartin, Joseph Jun.		1	3	Collections after sermons,	1	0	0
Hartin, Mrs. Joseph		1	3				
Hartin, Thomas Medley			7½		£8	5	2½

CHATHAM.

	£	s.	d.
Bacon, Rev. Samuel	£1	0	0
Burchell, George Jun.		5	0
Burchell, Mrs. George		5	0
Burchell, George Sen.		1	6
Blair, G. A.		5	0
Baldwin, Daniel		5	0
Baldwin, John		5	0
Baldwin, Alexander		5	0
Brehaut, Thomas Smith		5	0
Bell, John		5	0
Burr, John		5	0
Cunard, Henry	1	10	0
Carmichael, E. C. J.		5	0
Copping, Isaac		5	0
Cameron, Mary		1	3
Dunlap, William		5	0
Friend, A	1	0	0
Fealty, James		5	0
Flieger, John		5	0
Gillespie, Thomas F.		7	5
Gillespie, Mrs. Thomas F.		2	6
Gibbs, Arthur		5	0
Gremley, Charles		2	6
Harley, John		5	0
Hocken, Richard		5	0
Johnson, Hon. J. M.		10	0
Johnson, Mrs. E		10	0
Johnston, Mrs. William		5	0
Jackson, John		5	0
Jackson, Anthony		5	0
Letson, William		5	0
M'Culley, Caleb		5	0
M'Culley, Mrs. Caleb		5	0
M'Cullum, Louisa		2	6
Peters, Hon. Thomas H.	1	3	4
Parker, Miss		5	0
Parker, George		5	0
Parker, Mrs. George		5	0
Percival, John		5	0
Percival, Catherine		5	0
Palmer, Mrs. William		5	0
Powell, Miss		5	0
Parker, Edwin		5	0
Russell, John		5	0
Searle, Michael		5	0
Samuel, James		5	0
Smith, George		2	6
Trevors, David		5	0
Voudy, Thomas		5	0
Vanstone, Charles		5	0
Wright, John, 15s. omission last year,	1	15	0
Wright, Mrs.		10	0
Wright, Miss Amelia		10	0
Williston, John T.		5	0
Wilson, John		5	0
Winslow, Francis E.		5	0
Wilkinson, William		10	0
Wilkinson, Eliza Lovibond		10	0
Wilkinson, Eliza Bacon		5	0
Wilkinson, Wm. James	£0	5	0
Wilkinson, Mary Edith		5	0
Wilkinson, Aug. Thornton		5	0
June Collection,	3	1	6
	£24	10	1

DOUGLAS.

	£	s.	d.
Barker, Charles W. L.	£0	1	3
Brewer, Stephen G.		1	3
Brewer, Nathan		1	3
Brewer, Cornelius		1	3
Brewer, Mrs. Mary		1	3
Brewer, Anson		1	3
Brewer, David		1	3
Brewer, Abraham		1	3
Brewer, Mrs. Frances		1	3
Brewer, John Minor		1	3
Brewer, Mrs. Lucy		1	3
Burt, Abraham		2	6
Burt, A. T.		1	10½
Burt, Darius		2	6
Burt, Jeremiah		1	3
Burt, George		1	3
Burt, Jarvis		2	6
Curry, Mrs. William		2	6
Clanfield Henry		10	0
Close, Miss		2	6
Close, Mary		1	3
Crauss, Burden		1	3
Estey, Zebulon		1	3
Estey, Mrs. Elizabeth		1	3
Foshay, James		2	6
Foshay, Mrs. James		2	6
Foshay, Sylvester		2	6
Fowler, Stephen G.		2	6
Fowler, Charles H.		1	3
Fowler, Thomas		1	3
Fox, Edmund		2	6
Gascon, Mrs. and Jane		2	6
Hammond, Anne		10	0
Hill, Thomas		2	6
Jones, Mrs. John		2	6
Jones, Richard			7½
Jones, Aaron			7½
Lawrence, Thomas			7½
Lawrence, Moses		2	6
Lawrence, Jesse		1	3
Lawrence, Henry		2	6
Long, Captain George		10	0
Manson, Miss		7	6
M'Kay, Robert		1	3
M'Keen, Jacob		5	0
M'Keen, Mrs. Jacob		5	0
M'Keen, Mrs. George		5	0
M'Keen, Abraham		5	0
M'Keen, Mrs. Abraham		5	0
M'Nutt, Elizabeth		1	6
Morehouse, George		1	3
Morehouse, Zadoc		1	3
Morehouse, Elisha		1	3
Pidgeon, Mrs. George		5	0

	£	s	d
Pidgeon, Edward	£0	5	0
Roberts, Rev. G. G.	1	0	0
Roberts, J. C. Edward		2	6
Robinson, Colonel John	1	10	0
Robinson, Mrs. John		10	0
Robinson, Major William	1	0	0
Robinson, Hon. Frederick	1	0	0
Rogers, Jeremiah		2	6
Sloot, Robert		5	0
Sloot, Mrs. Robert		2	6
Sloot, Mrs. Benjamin		2	6
Smith, Samuel James		10	0
Smith, Joseph		5	0
Smith, J. E.		1	3
Stone, Aaron		1	3
Stone, Eben			7½
Thomas, William		1	3
Tomlinson, James		6	3
Tomlinson, Mrs. James		5	0
Tomlinson, Martha		2	1½
Tomlinson, Robert		2	6
Tomlinson, Jane		1	3
Waller, Henry		1	3
Waller, Purvis		2	6
Warren, Edith		1	3
Wright, Captain		6	3
Collections in Churches,	3	0	0½

£18 8 9½

FREDERICTON AND NEW MARYLAND.

FREDERICTON.

	£	s	d
Akerley, S. A.	£0	15	0
Allen, John C.		10	0
Beckwith, John A.		10	0
Bailey, Miss		5	0
Bedell, W. J.	1	0	0
Bedell, Mrs. W. J.		5	0
Bedell, Rankin		5	0
Black, Hon. William		10	0
Block, Alexander		5	0
Bird, C.		1	3
Carter, Hon. Chief Justice	5	0	0
Coster, Rev. C. G.		15	0
Cheyne, George R. N.		10	0
Cheyne, Miss		5	0
Campbell, G. M.	1	1	0
Cadwallader, William		2	6
Carman, William	1	0	0
Dibblee, Geo. J. and Mrs.		15	0
Emmerson, Mrs.		5	0
Eagan, William		5	0
Eggar, John		7	6
Fredericton, Bishop of	10	0	0
Fisher, Hon. C. and Mrs.	1	0	0
Fisher, Wm. and wife,		10	0
Fairweather, Miss		5	0
Graham, John		12	6
Grosvenor, William		15	0
Garden, Mrs.		1	3
Garden, James		1	3

	£	s	d
Garden, James Jun.	£0	2	6
Garden, Frank		2	6
Grant, Mrs.		1	3
Grant, Henry Ludlow		2	6
Gregory, John		10	0
Hopkins, Miss		10	0
Humphreys, —		2	6
Lee, Mrs. George	1	0	0
Lugrin, George		5	0
Lipsitt, A.		2	6
Manners Sutton, J. H. T.			
His Excellency the			
Lieut. Governor,	10	0	0
Medley, Charles		10	0
Mitchell, Alexander		10	0
Moore, Hugh		10	0
Moore, John	1	0	0
Miller, S. R.		10	0
Miller, Jacob		5	0
Morrow, Mary Ann		2	6
Odell, Hon. W. H.	1	0	0
Odell, Mrs. W. H.	1	0	0
Partelow, Hon. J. R.	1	0	0
Parker, Hon. N.	2	0	0
Parker, Miss		10	0
Phair, A. S.		5	0
Phair, W. B.	1	0	0
Paisley, W.		5	0
Priestley, George		5	0
Priestley, Mrs.		5	0
Quinn, W. H.		5	0
Roberts, George	1	0	0
Robb, James, M. D.		10	0
Robinson, W. H.	1	0	0
Ryan, Mrs.		2	1½
Ryan, John Jun.		2	6
Randolph, A. F.		10	0
Randolph, Mrs. A. F.		5	0
Simpson, John	1	0	0
Stratton, F. A. H. S.	1	0	0
Street, Hon. J. A.	1	5	0
Street, Mrs. J. A.		10	0
Street, Miss		5	0
Street, Sarah		5	0
Smith, Anthony		5	0
Seymour, Lydia		1	3
Shives, A. S.	1	0	0
Scott, Ann		2	6
Shore, Mrs.	1	0	0
Simonds, Edward	1	0	0
Simonds, Ann		2	6
Simonds, Henry		2	6
Thomas, John		15	0
Tilley, Hon. S. L.	2	0	0
Toldervy, Dr. and Mrs.		15	0
Wallace, George		5	0
Wallace, Charlotte		2	6
Wallace, Mary Ann		1	3
Wallace, Ann		1	3
Wilkinson, John	1	0	0
Woodman, Miss		2	6

Yardy, Edward   £0 5 0
June collec. in Cathedral, 17 16 5

£86 11 9½

NEW MARYLAND.

Dunbar, William   £0 3 1½
Fisher, Lewis   5 0
Fisher, Henry   5 0
Fisher, H. S.   1 3
Fisher, W. M.   1 3
Fletcher, Edward   2 6
Fletcher, Mrs. Edward   1 3
Fletcher, Rebecca   1 3
Graham, William   5 0
Hicklin, William   5 0
Hicklin, Mrs.   5 0
Horncastle, Joseph   5 0
Horncastle, Mrs. Joseph   2 6
Horncastle, W. C.   1 3
Horncastle, James   1 3
Lindsay, Mrs. J. M.   5 0
M'Knight, James   2 6
M'Knight, Mrs. James   1 6
M'Knight, Samuel   2 6
M'Knight, Mrs. Samuel   1 3
O'Leary, Mrs.   3 1½
Rice, David   1 3

£3 2 6

GAGETOWN.

Cooper, James   £0 2 6
Courtney, John   5 0
Currie, George   5 0
DeVeber, N. H.   1 0 0
DeVeber, James   5 0
Dinghee, Louis   2 6
DuVernet, H. J.   10 0
Gilbert, S. H.   15 0
Gilbert, Mrs.   5 0
Gilbert, the Misses   15 0
Gilchrist, Henry   2 6
Hamilton, John   2 6
Harding, C. A.   5 0
Hewlitt, G. (Hampstead),   10 0
Johnston, T. M.   5 0
Johnston, Mrs.   5 0
Knox, Frederick   5 0
Lyon, W. B.   2 6
Lyon, J. H.   2 6
M'Mulkin, —   2 6
M'Dermot, William   2 6
M'Dermot, Samuel   5 0
M'Allister, Archibald   5 0
Millidge, John   10 0
Neales, J. Stanley   2 6
Neales, Thomas   1 3
Neales, Henry   1 3
Neales, Mary   1 3
Neales, Helen   7½
Neales, Rose Stirling   7½

Peters, Henry, M. D.   £0 7 6
Rector,   10 6
Smith, D. S. & C. W.   15 0
Travis, J. W.   12 6
Tilley, Thomas   10 0
Tuck, Levi   2 6
Wetmore, Mrs. Chas. P.   10 0
Wetmore, Mrs. Robert   5 0
Watson, Mrs. W. S.   3 9
June semi-ann. collection, 2 5 9

£14 0 0

GREENWICH.

M'Leod, William Esq.   £0 5 0
M'Leod, Mrs.   2 6
Richards, W. D.   5 0
Wilmot, Mrs. J. M.   5 0
Wilmot, J. L. and Mrs.   12 6

£1 10 0

HAMPTON.

Bradwell, Robert (1858), £0 2 6
Fowler, Henry B.   5 0
Hayward, George (1858),   2 6
Smith, Newton   5 0
Price, William (1858,)   1 3
Wright, John H. "   10 0
Warrell, William "   5 0
Wilson, Robert "   5 0
June Collections, viz.:
Hampton,   4 10 0
Gondola Point,   2 1 6
French Village,   3 6 6

£11 14 3

HOPEWELL AND HARVEY.

Barberie, O   £0 5 0
Barberie, Mrs. O   2 6
Casey, W. H.   5 0
Dowling, Benjamin   5 0
Gilbert, Thomas   10 0
Gilbert, Mrs. T.   5 0
Hallett, William   5 0
Hallett, Mrs. William   2 6
Morse, S. G.   10 0
Morse, Mrs. A.   5 0
M'Kinley, J.   2 6
Nichols, Celia   7 6
Nichols, Amelia   5 0
Nichols, Rev. Henry B.   1 0 0
Rourk, William H.   5 0
Vickery, Miss   1 3
Coll. in Churches in June,   15 0

£5 11 3

KINGSCLEAR.

Black, Rev. J.   £1 0 0

Burnett, John	£0	3	1½	Northrup, James S.	£0	5	0
Clarkson, William		6	3	Northrup, Daniel		5	0
Dunphy, Thomas		3	1½	Northrup, Eli S.		5	0
Garden, George		10	0	Perkins, A. E. Esq.	1	0	0
Garden, James		2	6	Peters, Miss Amelia		15	0
Hartt, James		2	6	Pickett, A. Munson		2	6
Hay, Jane		1	3	Pickett, David		10	0
Hay, Mary A.			7½	Pickett, Horatio		2	6
Inches, Julius		10	0	Pickett, Justus		5	0
Kilner, Mrs. and family,		15	0	Puddington. J. W.		2	6
Lee, Mrs. T. C.		10	0	Raymond, William		5	0
Lee, John		5	0	Scovil, Mrs. and Miss	1	2	3
Lee, Thomas		5	0	Scovil, Rev. W. E.	1	0	0
Leek, George		2	6	Vail, Colonel J. C.	1	0	0
Leek, William		2	6	Wetmore, David Jun.		5	0
Murray, Isaac		10	0	Wetmore, David W.		5	0
Murray, Mrs. Isaac		5	0	Wetmore, E. Marshall		2	6
Murray, Jane		2	6	Wetmore, Justus S.	1	0	0
Murray, William		2	6	Wetmore, Justus		2	6
Murray, Mrs. Joseph		5	0	Whelpley, George F.		10	0
Maclauchlan, James A.		10	0	Whelpley, James		5	0
Nelson, James		5	0	Whiting, William		2	6
Parks, William		2	6	Whiting, Charles		2	6
Rainsford, A. W.		5	0	Collection,	5	0	0
Russell, Mrs.		2	10½				
Scovil, Mrs. S.		15	0		£22	0	0

	£8	4	9

LANCASTER.

Archibald, Miss	£0	5	0
Armstrong, John		2	6
A Friend,		1	3
Balcom, Allen J.		2	6
Balcom, Henry		2	6
Balcom, Joseph A.		5	0
Balcom, William		5	0
Bird, James		5	0
Bird, J. A. T.		2	6
Boggs, Mrs.		3	0
Briscoe, Charles		5	0
Brundage, Mrs.		3	0
Burke, T. E.		2	6
Carey, Robert		2	6
Carman, G. Clowes		10	0
Catherwood, Robert		1	3
Crockett, James		2	6
Cushing, Andrew		5	0
Donelly, James		2	6
Douglas, T.		1	3
Douglas, Elizabeth		1	3
Dunn, John		5	0
Dunn, R. C. J.		1	3
Ellman, William		10	0
Ellman, Mrs. William		10	0
Fair, Mrs.		2	6
Gamble, George		5	0
Garbutt, Henry	1	0	0
Garbutt, Mrs. Henry		5	0
Garbutt, Robert Wilson		2	6
Garbutt, Miss A. E. C.		2	6
Graham, Robert		2	6
Griffith, Edward		1	3

KINGSTON.

Appleby, John T.	£0	2	6
Black, Alexander	1	0	0
Brien, John		2	6
Chaloner, John		2	6
Crawford, Mrs. D.		1	3
Crawford, Frederick M.		5	0
Crawford, Mrs. Stephen		5	0
Dixon, John		5	0
Dixon, Thomas		4	0
Flewelling, Enos H.		2	6
Flewelling, Merritt		2	6
Flewelling, Robert J.		2	6
Flewelling, William J.		2	6
Flewelling, J. Bentley		2	6
Flewelling, Samuel E.		2	6
Foster, Howard		2	6
Foster, I. Hoyt		5	0
Foster, Samuel Esq.	1	5	0
Foster, Sophia		5	0
Gorham, N. R.		2	6
Hoyt, Samuel		5	0
Hoyt, Charles		5	0
Hoyt, Jarvis		5	0
Hoyt, George		2	6
Holder, Robert		2	6
Lyon, James B.		10	0
M'Alary, Alexander		2	6
M'Alary, Mrs. John		2	6
Nichols, Mrs. Charles		2	6
Nichols, Miss Jane		2	6
Nichols, Miss Phœbe		2	6

6

Griffith, James	£0 1 3
Hargrove, John	2 6
Hargrove, George	2 6
Hastings, Aaron	5 0
Haggard, Henry	2 6
Herricks, Richard	1 3
Herricks, Mrs.	1 3
Howard, Mrs. James	5 0
Jackson, Rev. W.	1 3
Jewitt, E. D.	1 0 0
Kemble, Richard	2 6
Kingston, Richard	5 0
Lawrence, Mrs.	1 3
Leslie, John	2 6
Littlehale, J. C.	5 0
Lord, John T.	5 0
Mason, Mrs.	5 0
Mackay, John	5 0
Mayo, Charles	5 0
Mewhenriey, Mrs. Wilson	2 6
Mills, William	1 3
Mills, Mrs. Mary	1 3
Molloy, Michael	1 3
Mount, Miss	5 0
M'Leod, Daniel	1 3
Nason, Mrs.	2 6
Noble, Mrs.	5 0
Odell, Thomas	2 6
Olive, Mrs. Isaac	5 0
Parker, Thomas	5 0
Quin, Henry	2 6
Quinton, James	10 0
Reed, Thomas	5 0
Reed, Thomas Jun.	2 6
Reed, James	5 0
Reed, James (2d)	2 6
Reed, Robert	2 6
Reed, David	2 5
Reed, George	5 0
Robinson, Miss	3 0
Rose, John	5 0
Roseborough, Rose	1 3
Scott, Mrs.	5 0
Shaw, Isaac	2 6
Smith, Robert	10 0
Smith, George F.	5 0
Smith, W. H.	5 0
Sutton, E.	10 0
Thompson, Richard	10 0
Thompson, Edward Sen.	1 3
Thompson, Edward Jun.	1 3
Thompson, William	2 6
Thompson, Martha	1 3
Thompson, Alice	1 3
Thorn, George	2 6
Tilton, John	5 0
Wetmore, S. T.	5 0
Wheaton, Edward	1 3
White, John	2 6
Yeats, Alexander	10 0

Sundry small sums,	£0 2 4
	£19 0 0

MAUGERVILLE AND BURTON.

MAUGERVILLE.

Bailey, Charles	£0 5 0
Bailey, Mrs. Charles	5 0
Bailey, Miss	2 6
Bailey, Charles William	5 0
Bailey, Thomas	2 6
Bell, Mrs.	5 0
Bent, Leonard	2 6
Bent, William	2 6
Clowes, John C.	10 0
Covert, George B.	5 0
Covert, John S.	5 0
Covert, Rev. W. S.	10 0
Currie, Charles D. O.	1 0 0
DeVeber, F. A.	10 0
DeVeber, Isaac	5 0
DeVeber, Miss	5 0
DeVeber, Duncan	5 0
DeVeber, William	5 0
Garrison, W. A.	5 0
Hatheway, C. L.	10 0
Hamilton, James	2 6
Miles, Mrs. Colonel	5 0
Miles, Thomas O.	5 0
Milner, Mrs.	5 0
Perley, Thomas H.	3 1½
Sheilds, Archibald	1 3
Street, Edwin	2 6
Sterling, D. A.	5 0
Sterling, Mrs. D. A.	5 0
Sterling, Archibald M'L.	5 0
Sterling, George A.	2 6
Sterling, A. A.	2 6
Taylor, Gain B.	3 1½
Wiggins, Rev. Dr.	1 0 0
June 25, 1st collection,	17 6
	£9 17 6

BURTON.

Beckwith, Thomas A.	£0 7 6
Bliss, George J.	1 0 0
Clowes, Charles H.	1 0 0
Clowes, Gerhardus	1 0 0
Gilbert, William I.	10 0
Gilbert, Samuel	10 0
Gilbert, John P.	10 0
Horton, Ebenezer	10 0
Hubbard, Nathaniel	1 0 0
Hubbard, M. J. E.	5 0
M'Clintock, Robert	10 0
M'Pherson, J. R.	2 6
White, James	10 0
Wilmot, Hon. R. D.	1 0 0
June 19, 1st collection,	1 8 2½
	£10 10 8½

NORTON.

Brown, James	£0	2	6
Bostwick, Mrs.		5	0
Cother, Thomas		5	0
Carney, Michael		2	0
Dixon, Charles	2	0	0
English, Mrs.		2	6
English, William		7	6
Earl, S. Z., M. D.		5	0
Earle, Thomas		2	0
Fairweather, Edwin		7	6
Fairweather, Mrs. E.		5	0
Fairweather, Julia		2	6
Fairweather, Isabella		2	6
Fairweather, Arthur		2	6
Fairweather, Kate		2	6
Fairweather, Samuel		5	0
Fairweather, Mrs. S.		5	0
Fairweather, Thos. and Mrs.		5	0
Fairweather, D. and Mrs.		5	0
Fairweather, O. and Mrs.		5	0
Fairweather, John and Mrs.		5	0
Fairweather, Jas. Albert		1	3
Fairweather, Allan Ernest		1	3
Fairweather, Miles J. G.		5	0
Fairweather, Miss Ann		2	6
Fairweather, James		10	0
Frost, Charles and Mrs.		5	0
Frost, Harvey and Mrs.		5	0
Frost, Miss		1	6
Frost, Miss Julia		1	6
Frost, Mrs.		2	6
Gedney, David		2	6
Gedney, Mrs. J.		2	6
Hendricks, C. J. and family,		10	0
Hughson, James		2	6
Hodges, Moses		2	6
Hoyt, Edwin and Mrs.	1	0	0
Hoyt, Mrs.		2	6
Hoyt, Mrs. Fanny		2	6
Hallett, James		5	0
Ketchum, William		2	6
Ketchum, Miss Hannah		2	6
Ketchum, Robert		2	6
Ketchum, Charles		2	6
Ketchum, Isaac		3	1
Ketchum, Peter		3	0
Ketchum, Mrs.		1	3
Ketchum, Miss Julia		1	3
Ketchum, T.' & C. and sister		7	6
Ketchum, Geo. and Mrs.		5	0
Leavitt, Mrs. J.		5	0
Lamoureux, G. T.		2	6
Piers, Robert J. and family,		2	6
Raymond, J.B.S. & family,	1	0	0
Raymond, the Misses		7	6
Rankin, Mrs.		5	0
Seely, Robert and Mrs.		7	6
Seely, Miss Mary Ann		1	3
Simonds, Rev. Richard	1	0	0
Simonds, Mrs. R.	1	0	0
Simonds, Lily	£0	5	0
Simonds, Cornelia		2	6
Simonds, Blanche		2	6
Simonds, James		2	6
Wetmore, H. S. and family,	1	0	0
Wetmore, E. S. Esq.		5	0
Wetmore, W. P.		3	0
Wetmore, Mrs. C. H. and family,		5	0
Wetmore, Norton and family,		5	0
Wetmore, J. Henry		1	3
Wetmore, Miss Susan E.		1	3
Collection in Church,		2	5	0

£19 9 10

PETERSVILLE.*

Armstrong, Rev. John	£1	0	0
Armstrong, John		5	0
Bayard, Dr. Sen.	1	0	0
Bayard, Charles		10	0
Bayard, Mrs.		5	0
Burgess, William		5	0
Burgess, Robert		5	0
Corbet, Andrew		2	6
Fowler, Thomas Sen.		5	0
Friend, A			7
Graham, Richard		10	0
Graham, Thomas		5	0
Hoffmann, Miss		?	0
Leonard, Thomas		5	0
Lyon, Richard		3	0
M'Kinney, Mr. Sen.		5	0
M'Kinney, William		5	0
Murray, Donald		5	0
Perkins, C. E.		5	0
Polly, James		5	0
Polly, Richard		5	0
Quin, James		5	0
Simpson, John		5	0
Smith, G.		1	0
Woods, Mr. Sen.		2	6
Woods, Francis		5	0
Collections,		2	10	0

£10 5 4

* The returns from this Parish, owing to a mistake, were not made in time to be included in the Report.

PRINCE WILLIAM, DUMFRIES, MAGUNDY, &c.

Allan, Miss	£0	1	6
Allan, Miss Ann		1	6
Atherton, Israel		1	3
Bain, John		2	6
Baker, Prince		5	0
Blaney, Henry		2	6
Brown, William		2	6
Brown, Henry		2	6
Brown, Thomas		5	0

	£	s	d
Brymer, Charles	£0	5	0
Charters, Edward		5	0
Charters, Robert		5	0
Close, Richard		2	6
Cunningham, James	1	0	0
Davidson, William		10	0
Davidson, John		5	0
Davidson, Mrs. John		5	0
Davidson, Mrs. Witter		7	6
Davis, Josiah		2	6
Edmondson, Isaac		2	6
Ellegood, Mrs.		3	1½
Ellegood, John		2	6
Ellegood, Mrs. John		2	6
Ellegood, William		5	0
Elliott, Thomas		7	6
Fraser, Thomas		5	0
Fraser, William		5	0
Fraser, Alexander		5	0
Fraser, George		2	6
Gartley, Peter		2	6
Gartley, John		2	6
Gartley, Andrew		1	3
Gartley, Letitia		2	6
Graham, Patrick		2	6
Graham, Gilbert		2	6
Graham, James		2	6
Hammond, Mrs. John		2	6
Harper, John		5	0
Henderson, James		2	6
Henry, Arthur		5	0
Henry, William		2	6
Henry, John Sen.		2	6
Henry, Mrs. John		2	6
Henry, John Jun.		2	6
Henry, John		5	0
Henry, James		5	0
Henry, Mrs. James		5	0
Henry, James Jun.		2	6
Henry, James Robert		2	6
Henry, William Jun.		2	6
Henry, Francis		2	6
Henry, Nelson		1	3
Holyoake, Mrs. Joseph		2	6
Hood, George		2	6
Hood, Frances		1	3
Jones, Thomas	1	0	0
Kilpatrick, John		2	6
King, Steward		2	6
Landers, Robert		2	6
Lockard, Benjamin		2	6
Lockard, Patrick		2	6
Lockard, Thomas		2	6
Long, Abraham		2	6
Loosemore, Rev. P. W.	1	0	0
Loosemore, Mrs.	1	0	0
Loosemore, Miss	1	0	0
Love, William		5	0
Love, George		2	6
Love, James		5	0
Love, Robert		5	0

	£	s	d
Love, Thomas	£0	5	0
Love, Joseph		2	6
Marshall, John		15	0
Miller, Robert		2	6
Miller, John		2	6
Miller, Arthur		5	0
Miller, William		5	0
Miller, Henry		2	6
M'Conaghy, James		3	0
M'Cormack, Charles		2	6
M'Cutcheon, Charles		2	6
M'Ilwain, Samuel		2	6
Nash, Mrs.		7	6
Nash, Miss		4	4½
Nash, Allan		3	1½
Noble, Robert		2	6
Smith, Mrs. Charles		2	6
Temple, Thomas		5	0
Whitehead, William		5	0
First collection,	2	3	1½
Second do.	2	0	0
	£24	4	9

QUEENSBURY.

	£	s	d
Brown, Mrs. A.	£0	7	6
Earls, Emily		5	0
Earls, Hester		5	0
Farmar, D. and sisters,		3	9
Hoyt, Joseph		5	0
Ingraham, Ira		7	6
Ingraham, Hannah		5	0
Ingraham, Benjamin		5	0
Ingraham, Mrs. B.		2	6
Ingraham, Henry		3	0
Ingraham, Charles		2	6
Ingraham, George		10	0
Miller, William		5	0
Movers, John		5	0
Morehouse, Charles		10	0
Prescote, William		2	6
Prescote, Thomas		2	6
Prescote, James		2	6
Stewart, Mrs.		3	1½
Stewart, Thomas S.		1	3
Tippet, Rev. Mr. and Mrs.	1	0	0
Tippet, Henry G.		12	3
Tippet, Vivian		1	3
Tippet, Mary V.		1	3
West, Ann		3	1½
June collection,		17	9
Proceeds of a box,		2	6
A thank offering,		2	6
	£7	14	3

SACKVILLE AND DORCHESTER.

SACKVILLE.

	£	s	d
Allison, Joseph F.	£2	0	0
Allison, H. B.		10	0
Anderson, Smith		2	6
Botsford, A. E.		10	0

	£	s	d
Botsford, George	£0	1	3
Boultenhouse, Ann		1	2½
Boultenhouse, Marrimettee		1	2½
Black, Samuel F.		5	0
Cogswell, Edward		5	0
Clark, James		2	5
Carson, John		2	6
Carson, Mrs.		1	3
Dixon, E. B.		2	6
DeWolf, Rev. T. N.	1	0	0
Evans, Miss Mary		1	3
Milner, Mrs. C.		2	6
M'Alister, Robert		1	2½
Palmer, Philip		5	0
Russ, Charles		2	6
Russ, Hazen		1	3
Robson, Thomas		10	0
Sinclair, Daniel		1	3
Sinclair, Mrs.		2	6
Wilkins, James		1	2½
Wilson, Rufus		1	3
Wilson, Richard		2	5
June collection,		16	0
	£7	13	2

DORCHESTER.

	£	s	d
Backhouse, William	£0	2	5
Botsford, Blair		5	0
Chapman, David		3	0
Chandler, E. B.	2	10	0
Gilbert, Bradford		10	4
Gilbert, Mrs. R. K.		5	0
Godfrey, Robert		5	0
Godfrey, Charles B.		3	9
Hickman, Joseph		3	0½
Hickman, John		3	0½
Hickman, William		2	5
Moore, J. L.		5	0
Palmer, Gideon		3	0
Smith, A. J.		5	0
Upham, J. E.		2	6
June collection,	2	3	5
	£7	11	11

ST. ANDREWS.

	£	s	d
Alley, Rev. Dr,	£0	5	0
Augherton, George		2	6
Augherton, Eliza		3	1½
Berry, Thomas		10	0
Berry, Thomas Jun.		5	0
Berry, Donald		5	0
Buck, Walter M.	1	0	0
Billings, Mary		5	0
Billings, Samuel		1	3
Billings, Mrs. Samuel		1	3
Billings, Richard			7½
Bradridge, Henry		5	0
Bell, James		2	6
Chandler, James W.		5	0
Campbell, George F.		5	0
Coughlan, Mrs.		5	0
Dimock, C. W.	£0	3	1½
Farmer, John		5	0
Gove, Dr.		5	0
Green, Captain		5	0
Grant, Alexander	1	0	0
Garden, H. M.		5	0
Gove, Mrs. C. M.	1	0	0
Hatch, H. H.	1	0	0
Hatch, Wellington		5	0
Hipwell, Thomas		5	0
Harvey, Hibbard		2	6
Jones, Thomas	1	0	0
James, R. D.		5	0
James, Mrs. R. D.		5	0
Johnston, Henry		2	6
Julian, Mrs.		10	0
Ketchum, Rev. W. Q.	1	0	0
Marsh, Mrs.	1	0	0
Miller, Robert		2	6
Moore, George		5	0
Mugford, Robert		2	6
Muir, Alexander		5	0
M'Kay, Gordon		2	6
M'Curdy, Stephen		1	3
Pheasant, Edward		5	0
Pheasant, Mrs.		2	6
Parkinson, John		5	0
Parkinson, A. T.		2	6
Rainsford, M.		5	0
Rankin, Mrs.			7½
Street, James W.	1	0	0
Street, George D.	1	0	0
Street, John A. Jun.		5	0
Street, Maria		5	0
Street, Helen		5	0
Street, Herbert		1	3
Smith, John		5	0
Smith, Rev. R. E.		10	0
Slason, William		5	0
Stone, Mrs.		5	0
Storr, Mrs.		2	6
Shaw, Mrs. Robert		1	3
Shaw, Margaret		1	3
Shaw, Mary Ann		1	3
Stinson, Mary		1	3
Stickney, George F.		5	0
Thompson, Captain		10	0
Thompson, Julius		10	0
Turner, Mrs.		2	6
Treadwell, Nathan		2	6
Whitlock, William	1	0	0
Whitlock, J. H.		5	0
Wilson, Edward		5	0
Wilson, John D.		5	0
Wardlaw, C. W.		5	0
Wardlaw, Mrs.		5	0
Wilson, T. B.		2	6
Wilson, Mrs. T. B.		2	6
Collection after sermon,	9	6	5
Do. in Chamcook,	1	6	0
	£33	19	11

ST. DAVID AND ST. PATRICK.

	£	s	d
Acheson, James	£0	2	6
Acheson, Mrs. James		2	6
Acheson, William		2	6
Acheson, Mrs. William		2	6
Acheson, William Jun.		5	0
Bell, Thomas Jun.		5	0
Blackwood, Miss Amanda		2	6
Black, Mrs.		2	6
Black, Miss Jane		2	6
Black, Miss M.		1	3
Black, Charles		1	3
Carter, Nicholas		3	9
Carter, James Jun.		3	9
Cameron, Miss Robenia		1	3
Coulter, James		2	6
Dacon, Joseph		5	0
Dyer, Richard		2	6
Dyer, Mrs. Richard		2	6
Doore, Stephen		2	6
Doore, Mrs. Jane		1	3
Duplassey, William		2	6
Duplassy, Mrs.		2	6
Hill, John		2	6
Hill, Mrs. John		2	6
Hadley, Obadiah		5	0
Irvin, John		5	0
Irvin, William		2	6
Kirkwood, Thomas		2	6
Powers, Warren		2	6
Powers, Miss Clarissa		2	6
Powers, Thaddeus B.		2	6
Powers, Frederick H.		1	3
Regan, Mrs. John		3	9
Scott, Samuel		5	0
Scott, Miss Vashti I.		2	6
Scott, Theodore		2	6
Sherman, Valentine		2	6
Sherman, Mrs. Valentine		2	6
Smith, Mrs. Mary		4	6
Thomson, Rev. J. S.		10	0
Thompson, Frederick		3	9
Thompson, Mrs. Frederick		2	6
Thompson, James		2	6
Towers, William		2	6
Towers, Mrs. William		2	6
Towers, Miss Margaret		1	3
Towers, George		1	3
Towers, Robert		1	3
Towers, Robert Sen.		2	6
Towers, Mrs. Robert		2	6
Towers, John		2	6
Towers, Mrs. John		2	6
Wills, John		2	6
Wills, Mrs. John		2	6
	£7	4	6

ST. GEORGE AND PENNFIELD.

	£	s	d
Adams, Mrs. S.	£0	5	0
Andrews, Miss J.		2	6

	£	s	d
A Church lady,	£0	2	6
Brown, James		2	6
Crickett, John		1	3
Cluff, Matthew		1	3
Eldridge, Sarah		1	3
Gillespie, James		2	1
Hatheway, Mrs.		2	6
Hunter, Mrs.		1	3
Johnson, Samuel		5	0
Johnson, Charles		2	6
Justason, Isaac		2	6
Knight, Gideon		5	0
Knight, Mrs. J.		3	1½
Knight, E. P.		1	3
Knight, J. E.		2	6
Knight, George		2	6
Ludgate, Hugh		5	0
Murphy, Henry		2	6
Messinett, Claudius		5	0
M'Callum, Hugh		2	6
M'Givern, Rev. J.		10	0
M'Master, Captain A. D.		8	1½
M'Gee, Richard		5	0
M'Gee, Richard Jun.		2	6
M'Carty, Richard		5	0
M'Carty, Henry		2	6
Randall, Benjamin		5	0
Randall, Mrs.		5	0
Sherrard, John		2	6
Thomson, Rev. S.	1	0	0
Thomson, Mrs.		10	0
Wetmore, A. J. W.		5	0
Wetmore, Mrs.		5	0
Wetmore, Douglas		2	6
Williams, Mrs. Phœbe		5	0
Wood, Adam		2	6
Walls, Richard Charles		1	3
Col. in St. Mark's, June 19,	1 14	4½
Do. do.		11	0½
	£10	3	9

SIMONDS.

	£	s	d
Armstrong, R. Sands	£0	10	0
Armstrong, James		2	6
Armstrong, William		2	6
Armstrong, John		2	6
Armstrong. Mrs. John		1	3
Burns, John		2	6
Burke, John		2	6
Daly, William		3	9
Evans, William		2	6
Evans, Mrs. William		1	6
Evans, Robert		2	6
Evans, Mrs. Robert		1	3
Evans, Richard		3	0
Evans, Mrs. Richard		2	0
Lynch, Hugh,		2	6
Lynch, James K.		1	3
Moore, John		2	6
Moore, Mrs. John		2	6

	£	s	d			£	s	d
Moore, Robert	£0	2	6	Besnard, Mr. and Mrs. P.	£1	0	0
Scott, William		2	6	Boyd, Henry C.		5	0
Jordan, John Sen.		2	6	Brown, John C.		5	0
Jordan, John Jun.		2	6	Bryant, J. P.		2	6

*£2 19 0

* This amount is less than that first reported.

ST. STEPHEN.

	£	s	d			£	s	d
Abbott, P. M.	£0	5	0	Card, Henry		10	0
Abbott, Mrs.		2	6	Christian, Thomas	2	0	0
Abbott, Miss Mary C.		1	3	Cudlip, John W.	1	0	0
Abbott, Miss S. H.		1	3	Cutler, James E.		5	0
Atherton, Mrs.		2	6	Daley, Paul		2	8
Andrews, Mrs. W.		1	10½	Davidson, William	1	0	0
Bixby, Mrs.		2	6	DeVoe, John D.		10	0
Bixby, Miss S.		2	6	Dolby, Mrs. Edward		10	0
Blair, Mrs.		6	3	Duffill, William		5	0
Bolton, J.		5	0	Frost, John		5	0
Bolton, Mrs.		3	1½	Hall, Mrs.	1	0	0
Grimmer, J.		10	0	Hammond, Mrs. William		5	0
Grimmer, George S.		10	0	Hanford, J. T. and Mrs.	2	0	0
Grimmer, W. W.		3	1½	Hardenbrook, John		5	0
Johnson, W.		2	6	Howard, James	1	0	0
Lindsay, Ninian		5	0	Johnston, Mrs. Hugh	3	0	0
Lindsay, Mrs. N.		2	6	Johnston, Miss A.	2	0	0
Lindsay, Mrs. R.		5	0	Johnston, Miss	2	0	0
Marks, Mrs. Nehemiah		7	6	Kerr, John	2	0	0
M'Kewen, Mr.		5	0	Kirkpatrick, Charles	1	0	0
Porter, Mrs. B.		2	6	Lawrence, G. H.		10	0
Porter, James		10	0	Lawton, William G.	1	0	0
Porter, Mrs. Joseph		2	6	Lordly, A. J.		6	1
Pollard, Rev. H.	1	0	0	Magee, Abraham		5	0
Rose, David A.		7	6	Majoribanks, Thomas		5	0
Rose, J. H.		2	6	Matthew, George		10	0
Rose, Mrs. J. H.		2	6	Melick, Charles J.		10	0
Sands, George E.		5	0	Melick, Henry		10	0
Smith, Mrs. E.		2	6	Merritt, E. Miles		5	0
Smith, Thomas		2	6	Merritt, Mrs. Thomas	1	5	0
Springate, Edward		5	0	Merritt, Miss Susan		3	0
Stewart, Miss		5	0	Merritt, Miss Ann C.		3	0
Thomson, Rev. Dr.	1	5	0	Merritt, Gray T.		3	0
Thomson, George	1	0	0	Merritt, David P.		3	0
Thompson, Miss K.		3	1½	Merritt, Albert		3	0
Verome, William		2	6	Magee, John		10	0
Waddell, James		7	6	Merritt, Charles	2	10	0
Watson, Robert	1	0	0	M'Givern, R. P.		10	0
Watson, William		3	1½	Macdonald, Mrs. C. C.		10	0
Webber, Henry		5	0	M'Grath, John	1	0	0
Webber, Mrs. H.		3	6	M'Nichol, J.		5	0
				M'Nichol, J. Jun.		5	0
£12 1 7½				Nicholson, John W.	2	0	0
				Parker, Hon. Judge	10	0	0
SAINT JOHN—TRINITY.				Patton, Charles	1	0	0
Allison, Edward	£0	10	0	Patton, Thomas		5	0
Allison, Edward Jun.		10	0	Perkins, James D.		5	0
Almon, L. J.	1	5	0	Powers, M. N.		10	0
Ballentine, Alexander		5	0	Pickup, W. D.		10	0
Bayard, Robertson	2	0	0	Rhynd, Robert		5	0
Beacoll, George B.		5	0	Ranney, Henry		5	0
Beard, J. W.		10	0	Rawleigh, Mrs.	3	0	0
Bentley, Miss		10	0	Robinson, Beverley	5	0	0
				Sandall, John		5	0
				Savary, A. W.		5	0
				Scammell, Joseph		10	0
				Sancton, Thomas A.	1	0	0

Scovil, Rev. Wm. (for Widow and Orphan Fund),	£5	0	0
Scoullar, George		5	0
Sears, Edward	1	0	0
Sears, John		6	8
Simonds, Miss	5	0	0
Smith, Edward		5	0
Stone, John		7	6
Sturdee, Henry P.	1	4	4
Spurr, James DeW.	1	0	0
Thomson, Miss	1	0	0
Tilton, John		10	0
Thurger, John V.	5	0	0
Trinity Sunday School,	2	4	3
Wetmore, O. D.		5	0
Whitney, G. W.		15	0
Wigglne, Stephen	100	0	0
Wiggins, F. A.	20	0	0
Woolan, B. M.		5	0
Walton, W.		5	0
Wedderburn, William	1	4	4
Weldon, Charles W.	2	10	0
Woodward, Isaac		10	0
Whitney, James A.		10	0
Col. in Trinity Church,	19	17	6
	£235	5	5

ST. JOHN—ST. JAMES.

Abell, Mrs.	£0	2	6
Agar, Mrs.		1	3
Andrews, D.		2	6
Armstrong, Rev. W.	4	0	0
Armstrong, Mrs. W.	2	0	0
Bates, Mrs.		5	0
Betts, Captain H.		5	0
Blake, John		1	3
Blake, Mrs.		1	3
Boyd, Mrs.	1	0	0
Brakey, Mrs.		2	6
Brittain, Mrs.		5	0
Brown, Mrs.	1	4	6
Brown, Mrs. J.		1	3
Burns, Mrs.		1	6
Bunworth, Miss		2	6
Cairns, W.		2	6
Carey, Captain R. A.		5	0
Cassidy, Richard		5	0
Cassell, Mrs.		1	3
Cash,		5	0
Children Parish Sunday School,	1	10	0
Chubb, Mrs.		5	0
Clark, Miss		1	3
Clark, James		2	6
Connolly, R.		1	3
Crockford, J.		5	0
Crookshank, R. W.		10	0
Crookshank, R. W. Jun	4	0	0
Crookshank, Miss		10	0
Crookshank, Miss J.		7	6

DeForest. S. J.	£0	2	6
Dibblee, F.		2	0
Dibblee, N.		3	0
Dickson, D.		1	6
Dickson, Miss		5	0
Dobbin, Mrs.		1	3
Donald, Mrs.		5	0
Donaghey, W.		2	6
Dorrethy, Mrs.		1	3
Ellis, Mrs.		5	0
Elward, James		7	6
Emison, W.		2	6
Farmer, Mrs.		1	3
Fenety, G. E.		5	0
Fletcher, Henry		5	0
Fletcher, Mrs.		2	6
Friend,		5	0
Frith, H. W.	2	0	0
Frith, F. C. K.		10	0
Foster, S. K.		10	0
Follis, William		5	0
Follis, John		2	6
Gordon, Mrs.		5	0
Godsoe, W. C.		10	0
Gossett, Major R. E.		10	0
Grant, Mrs.		1	3
Grant, J. M., R. E. Dept.	1	0	0
Green, —		1	3
Griffin, Mrs.		1	3
Griffiths, Mrs.		2	6
Hall, J. T.		7	6
Hare, Miss		12	6
Harris, H.		1	3
Hill, Jno.		1	3
Holden, Mrs.		5	0
Horner, William		5	0
Howard, Mrs.		1	3
Howard, A.		2	5
Humphrey, Mrs.		2	6
Hutchison, James		2	6
Huyghue, S. (War Dept.)		5	0
Hunter, R.		5	0
Isaacs, Mrs.		5	0
Jordan, D.		10	0
Jordan, F. G.		5	0
Jordan, W.		5	0
Kay, Captain		1	3
Kee, Mrs. George		5	0
Kee, W.		5	0
Kee, John		3	0
Kee, Thomas		2	6
Kee, George		5	0
Kinnear, Mrs. J.		2	6
Kinnear, Miss E.		2	6
Knoulton, Mrs.		5	0
Larkins, Mrs.		5	0
Lawson, Mrs.		3	0
Leavitt, Mrs.		1	3
Leonard, Mrs.		2	6
Lowry, John		2	6
Lowry, William		2	6

Name	£	s	d
Marshall, Mrs.	£0	5	0
Magee, Mrs. R.		1	3
Member of the Church,		10	0
Millidge, Miss	1	0	0
Morris, W. J.		1	3
Morris, Mrs.		1	3
Moulson, John		2	6
Nagle, W.		5	0
Neil, W. H.		1	3
Nethery, James		2	6
Nethery, Mrs.		1	3
North, John		2	6
Paterson, Mrs.		1	3
Parsons, Mrs.		3	0
Partelow, Charles		5	0
Paul, Mrs.		1	8
Peel, Mrs.		1	6
Peel, Mrs. H.		3	9
Perrin, S.		2	6
Peters, B. L.	2	10	0
Pengilly, R.		2	6
Pike, Mrs.		10	0
Phillips, R.		1	3
Portmore, Mrs. J.		5	0
Porter, Mrs.		5	0
Price, James		7	6
Reynard, James		5	0
Riley, Mrs.		1	0
Riley, John		2	3
Riddle, Thomas		1	3
Rhynd, Mrs.		2	6
Robinson, J. M. and Mrs.	5	0	0
Robinson, Mrs. W. H.	5	0	0
Sage, James		7	6
Sage, H. E.		5	0
Sage, James, Jun.		2	6
Sandall, John		2	6
Scovil, S. J.	1	5	0
Scovil, Mrs. S. J.	1	5	0
Scribner, Mrs.		1	3
Seeds, Samuel		5	0
Sharp, Mrs.		5	0
Sheridan, P.		1	3
Sheridan, Mrs.		1	3
Sherrard, Mrs.		2	6
Simpson, Mrs.		1	5
Smith, W.		2	6
Smith, M. B.		7	6
Smith, Mrs.		1	3
Spain, Mrs.		5	0
Starr, R. Peniston		10	0
Stewart, James		5	0
Stewart, W. O.		5	0
Stewart, D.		1	3
Stewart, E.		1	3
Sulis, C. E.		1	3
Sulis, Mrs. George		5	0
Sulis, Joseph		5	0
Sulis, Mrs. Thomas		2	0
Swinney, Miss	1	0	0
Tapp, W. H. (War Dept.)	1	4	6

7

Name	£	s	d
Thomas, Mrs.	£0	1	3
Thompson, John		10	0
Trentowsky, A. C. O.		10	0
Wagstaff, Miss		2	6
Weldon, J. W.	2	10	0
Wetmore, A. R.	1	5	0
Wetmore, Mrs. A. R.	1	5	0
Whitley, Mrs.		5	0
Wilson, Thomas		5	0
Wilson, John		5	0
Woodburn, Mrs.		1	8
Woodley, Mrs.		1	8
Wright, William	10	0	0
Wright, John	1	0	0
Collection in Church,	4	5	0
	£83	1	7

ST. JOHN—ST. MARK'S.

Name	£	s	d
Adams, W. H.	£3	0	0
Armstrong, Rev. G. M.	1	0	0
Armstrong, Mrs. G. M.		12	6
Armstrong, John S.		5	0
Armstrong, Mary A.		2	6
Armstrong, W. H.		2	6
Avery, W. L.		5	0
Anderson, Isaac		5	0
Adams, A.		5	0
Armstrong, John		7	6
Anning, John		5	0
Anning, George		2	6
Bentley, Miss		10	0
Bonsall, Miss		10	0
Bunting, Mrs. R.		5	0
Blatch, George		7	6
Berton, S. D.	2	0	0
Berton, Mrs. S. D.		10	0
Berton, Miss		5	0
Berton, W. S.		2	6
Barlow, Mrs.		5	0
Barlow, Miss Helen		5	0
Barlow, Miss Jane		5	0
Benill, Mrs.			7
Brookins, Mrs.		2·6	
Boyne, Thomas		5	0
Beatteay, Dr.		5	0
Chipman, Mrs.	5	0	0
Crawford, W. K.		5	0
Clark, Miss L. A.		5	0
Clements, W. N. H.		3	0
Clementson, Francis	1	0	0
Coughlin, A. A.		10	0
Crozier, Thomas		10	0
Clinch, T. R.		10	0
Cutler, R. T.		7	0
Campbell, C.		2	6
Caldwell, David		10	0
Cunningham, Thomas		5	0
DeVeber, L. H.	3	0	0
DeVeber, Mrs. L. H.	1	0	0
DeVeber, R. S.	1	0	0
DeVeber, Boies	1	0	0

Name	£	s	d	Name	£	s	d
Dickson, Charles T.	£0	5	0	Kinnear, C. F.	£0	5	0
Daniel, T. W.	5	0	0	Kollock, Miss		10	0
Dole, W. P.		10	0	Keans, W. H. A.		10	0
DeForest, G. F.		10	0	Keans, George F.		2	6
Disbrow, Mrs. N.		19	6	Lester, J. G.		5	0
Daniel, Arthur		10	0	Lester, W. H.		5	0
Daniel, Mrs. Arthur		5	0	Lee, Miss		5	0
Dickson, R. S.	1	0	0	Lee, Robert		5	0
Dickson, Mrs. R. S.		5	0	Lordley, Joseph		5	0
Davidson, Mrs.		5	0	Lawrence, Joseph		10	0
Emery, Oliver		5	0	Larkins, Captain C.		5	0
Elliott, —		5	0	Mills, William		15	0
Evans, Evan		5	0	Milton, Mrs.		1	3
Foster, C. V.		10	0	Minnette, R. C.		5	0
Foster, Mrs. C. V.		5	0	M'Carty, Michael		10	0
Foster, Dr. A. T. D.		10	0	M'Avity, John		10	0
Foster, Mrs. A. T. D.		5	0	M'Avity, Mrs. A.		5	0
Flood, Carson		5	0	M'Gowan, John		5	0
Foster, Ankey		5	0	M'Dougall, Mrs.		5	0
Foster, Mrs. Ankey		2	6	Nagy, Daniel		5	0
Foster, M. J.		1	3	Olson, James		10	0
Foster, Roxanna		1	3	Perkins, D. C.	1	0	0
Foster, Isabella		1	3	Perkins, Harvey		5	0
Foster, Amelia		1	3	Perkins, Mrs. H.		2	6
Fairweather, C. H.	2	10	0	Perkins, Mrs. Mary		5	0
Fairweather, Mrs. C. H.	1	0	0	Perkins, Mrs. A. S.		5	0
Fairweather, F. R.		5	0	Peters, Mrs. Ann		5	0
Fairweather, L. S.		5	0	Price, Benjamin		5	0
Garnett, William		5	0	Peters, Mrs. C. I.	1	0	0
Grindon, T. E.		5	0	Peters, Hurd	1	0	0
Gibbon, W. H.		5	0	Peters, E. B.		5	0
Gillis, John	2	10	0	Ruel, James R.	1	0	0
Green, James		3	0	Robilliard, Agnes		5	0
Horsfall, James		10	0	Ritchie, William		4	6
Henderson, Matthew		3	0	Ritchie, Mrs. William		2	6
Holmes, —		5	0	Rhodes, Mrs.		5	0
Hubbard, W. D. W.		5	0	Secord, J. F.		5	0
Hubbard, Miss S. W.		2	6	Secord, Mrs. J. F.		5	0
Hubbard, W. W.		2	6	Seely, Miss		1	3
Hubbard, Miss H.		5	0	Smith, T. M.		15	0
Hutchinson, Mrs. William		2	6	Smith, William F.		10	0
Hatheway, Mrs. T. G.		10	0	Street, W. H.		5	0
Howard, D. S.		10	0	Stubbs, R.		5	0
Hall, S. S.	5	0	0	Scribner, P. B.		5	0
Hastings, J.		5	0	Tisdale, T. E. G.	1	0	0
Hooke, G. E.		2	6	Thomson, Joseph		5	0
Hazen, Miss	1	0	0	Thorne, E. L.		10	0
Heiber, Jacob		5	0	Taylor, J. P.		5	0
Irish, J. W. M.		5	0	Turner, J. D.		10	0
Irish, Mrs. J. W. M.		5	0	Turner, Mrs. J. D.		5	0
Jarvis, Mrs. William	1	0	0	Turner, Miss Ida		5	0
Jarvis, William M.		10	0	Turnbull, W. W.		10	0
Jones, Simeon		7	6	Tucker, C. H.		5	0
Keator, James	1	0	0	Vroom, W. E.		10	0
Keator, Mrs.		10	0	Whelpley, W. W.		10	0
Keator, Dr.	1	0	0	Waterbury, Mrs.		5	0
Kaye, J. J.	1	0	0	Winters, John		5	0
Kaye, Dorothy		2	6	Ward, John	1	0	0
Ketchum, Mrs. E.		5	0	Ward, Charles	1	0	0
Kenna, Mrs.		2	6	Collection,	10	12	9
Kenna, Miss		2	6				
Ketchum, F.		5	0		£97	13	10

ST. PAUL'S—PORTLAND.

	£	s	d
Adams, John	£0	5	0
Andrews, Mrs.		2	6
Armstrong, Robert		2	6
Armstrong, Edward		2	6
Armstrong, Christopher		2	6
Besnard, Peter Jun.		2	6
Brown, Edward		5	0
Burtis, W. R. M.		10	0
Boyd, J. Edward	1	0	0
Carman, W. H.		10	0
Carman, Mrs. W. H.		10	0
Coster, Miss		5	0
Cochrane, John		5	0
Crowley, John		5	0
Davison, William		2	6
Drury, Mrs.	1	5	0
Drury, Miss		5	0
Drury, Charles		10	0
Drury, W. C. and Mrs.	2	0	0
Fairweather, Joseph	1	0	0
Fairweather, George E.	2	0	0
Fairweather, Edwin	1	5	0
Fairweather, Thomas	1	0	0
Fuge, F. E.	1	4	4
Garby, George		5	0
Howe, John	1	0	0
Jack, William	1	0	0
Jack, J. Allen	1	0	0
Jackson, John		1	3
Lee, Rev. C.		10	0
Lee, W. T. P.	1	0	0
Light, Alexander L.	2	0	0
Luckie, C. E.	1	0	0
Manks, F.		5	0
Mount, Mrs.		5	0
Mount, Miss		2	6
Patterson, J. G.		2	6
Patterson, Mrs. J. G.		2	6
Payne, Robert		10	0
Payne, Isabella R.		5	0
Payne, William R.		3	0
Peacock, Eliza		2	6
Peters, E. B.	1	0	0
Peters, Miss	1	0	0
Peters, James W.		10	0
Peters, William T.	1	0	0
Peters, A. W.		5	0
Ramsay, David	• 2	6	
Ramsay, Rebecca		2	6
Ritchie, Hon. W. J.	4	0	0
Rowe, John S.		5	0
Rowling, John		2	6
Scovil, W. H.	5	0	0
Smith, H. B.	2	0	0
Smith, G. Sidney		10	0
Snider, George E.	1	0	0
Snider, George H.		5	0
Street, W. W.		10	0
Taylor, John		5	0
Thomson, S. R.	2	0	0

	£	s	d
Thompson, Susan	£0	5	0
Thorne, J. Scovil		5	0
Tucker, J.		5	0
Wetmore, T. S.	1	0	0
Wetmore, H. G. C.		5	0
Wright, Arthur		10	0
Collection, 12th June.	5	7	2
	£52	8	3

SUSSEX.

	£	s	d
Arnold, O. Roswell	£1	0	0
Arnold, Nelson Esq.	1	0	0
Arnold, Mrs. N.		5	0
Arnold, Thomas O.		5	0
Arnold, Mrs. T. O.		2	6
Arnold, T. Oliver Esq.		10	0
Arnold, George S.		5	0
Arnold, William R.		5	0
Arnold, Mrs. William R.		5	0
Arnold, William S.		2	6
Barnes, George		5	0
Beer, Captain (R. N.)	1	0	0
Beer, Edwin B.		15	0
Beer, Miss Mary		2	6
Beer, Miss Jane		2	6
Cougle, Mrs. K.	•	10	0
Cougle, William H.		2	6
Crawford, Edwin	1	0	0
Crawford, Mrs. E.		2	6
DeMill, Abraham		5	0
Dykeman, Jacob W.		5	0
Ellison, Robert		5	0
Ellison, George		2	6
Ellison, Mrs. George		2	6
Ellison, George Jun.		2	6
Evanson, A. C. Esq.		5	0
Evanson, Mrs.		5	0
Fairweather, George M.		10	0
Fairweather, Mrs. G. M.		5	0
Fairweather, Douglas		5	0
Fairweather, Miss		2	6
Flewelling, Reuben		5	0
Flewelling, Ezekiel		5	0
Friend, A.		2	6
Frazee, Rachel		2	6
Hallett, Oliver		5	0
Hallett, Mrs. Oliver		5	0
Hallett, Joseph		10	0
Hallett, James M.		2	6
M'Elliman, A. T. D.		5	0
M'Ghee, Rev. T.	1	0	0
M'Ghee, Mrs.		5	0
Ogilvie, John		5	0
Parlee, Mrs. John		2	6
Parlee, Henry		2	6
Parlee, Wellesley		2	6
Parlee, Edmund		1	3
Smith, Thomas		10	0
Smith, William		10	0
Sharp, Robert S.		3	0½

Sharp, Mrs. Robert S.	£0	2	6	Fletcher, William H.	£0	5	0
Snider, George		3	0½	Foster, Robert		5	0
Snider, Mrs. George		3	0½	Foster, Samuel		2	6
Snider, Xenophon		7	6	Fowler, Henry		7	6
White, Hiram		10	0	Fowler, James M.		10	0
White, George		5	0	Fowler, Daniel		10	0
Vail, Dr. E. A.		10	0	Fowler, Joseph A.		10	0
Vail, Mrs. E. A.		5	0	Fowler, Mrs. William M.		5	0
Vail, Miss		2	6	Fowler, Henry G.		8	0
Vail, Herbert		2	6	Fowler, Noah		2	6
Prayer Books sold,		5	0	Fowler, Elizabeth Ann		2	6
Collection, June 19,	1	14	9½	Fowler, Victoria		2	6
Do. at Portage Church,	2	10	0	Fowler, Emmeline		2	6
				Hanlyn, Samuel		2	6
	£23	0	2	Hanlyn, Joseph		2	6
				Harvey, James		2	6
UPHAM, HAMMOND, AND ST.				Hemphill, Michael		5	0
MARTIN'S.				Hodgin, John		8	0½
A Friend,	£0	3	0½	Ireland, Robert		2	6
A Churchwoman,		3	0½	Kilpatrick, Mrs.		2	6
Barlow, William		1	3	Kilpatrick, John		1	3
Connors, James		2	6	Kilpatrick, James		1	3
Chambers, Thomas		2	6	Kilpatrick, Ann		1	3
Debow, William		5	0	Kilpatrick, Martha		1	3
Debow, Mrs.		1	3	Lackie, Samuel		2	6
Debow, Stephen		6	0	Lackie, Robert		2	6
Debow, Charles		2	6	Lefurgey, Isaac		1	3
Debow, Richard		2	6	Marshall, William		5	0
Debow, James		2	6	M'Intosh, Hugh		5	0
DeMill, Henry		5	0	Scott, William		5	0
DeMill, Mrs. Henry		5	0	Sherwood, Mrs.		10	0
DeMill, Charles		5	0	Sherwood, John F.		7	6
DeMill, Mrs. Charles		5	0	Smith, Edward		5	0
DeMill, James W.		10	0	Smith, Caleb		2	6
DeVeber, Rev. W. H.	2	0	0	Upham, Joshua		10	0
Dodge, Isaac A.		5	0	Upham, Jabez		10	0
Dodge, Mrs. Isaac A.		5	0	Upham, James		10	0
Dodge, Charles		1	3	Upham, J. Cutler		10	0
Dodge, Fanny		1	3	Upham, Nathaniel		5	0
Drummond, William		5	0	Walker, Mrs. James		10	0
Drummond, Mary		2	6	Walker, Margaret		5	0
Drummond, Thomas		8	0½	Walker, Eliza		5	0
Drummond, David		1	4	Wanamake, Mrs.		5	0
Drummond, Margaret		1	3	Wanamake, N. Pickle		3	0½
Douglas, Henry		10	0	Collection in Church,	1	18	11
Douglas, James		5	0	A thank offering,	5	0	0
Fenwick, Ezekiel		3	0½				
Fletcher, George		2	6	*£25	0	0

* The Missionary was unavoidably prevented from calling upon many of the annual subscribers, whose names would otherwise have appeared in the above list.

APPENDIX.

DIOCESAN CHURCH SOCIETY OF NEW BRUNSWICK.

THE Anniversary Meeting of the Diocesan Church Society was held at Fredericton. on Thursday the 7th July, 1859. His Excellency Sir H. T. Manners Sutton, Governor of the Province, in the Chair.

Prayers were offered as usual, and a hymn was sung, when his Excellency addressed the meeting as follows :

In opening the proceedings of this meeting, I am very well aware that it would be wholly unnecessary, and worse than useless, for me to occupy your time in attempting to advocate the claims of the Church Society to your support, and that of every member of the Church of England in this Province. I know that these claims are generally understood and recognized. But I may perhaps say for myself, that having been near five years a member of this Society, a close observer of its proceedings, and the effects which it has produced throughout the Province, every succeeding year has caused, in my mind, an increasing appreciation of its value. Not only because it affords the channel and the means by which a very large and increasing portion of those pecuniary means, upon which the Church of England here has mainly to depend, flows, but also, because it is the link (a strong link, a close link) of union between the clergy and the laity: a link of union which, humanly speaking, affords the only prospect of peace within the church, and which (in my opinion at least) is the strongest power within the natural reach of man for the preservation of religion. These then are the reasons, and I have stated them shortly, not because I wish to put myself forward as the advocate of a society whose claims to your support are known and acknowledged, but I have thought it right on this occasion, after five years experience, to pay my tribute of gratitude to the society. It is not within the scope of my functions on this occasion, nor would it be consistent with my duty in opening the proceedings of this meeting, to forestall the Secretary in the Report which he is about to read to you, but there is one single point upon which, without entering into particulars, I may be allowed to offer some observations. This is by anticipation, rather than retrospect, the anniversary meeting of the Society. Six months only have elapsed since another anniversary meeting took place. It might naturally be supposed that the shortness of the period which had elapsed since the last collection would have had a very detrimental effect on the amount of the contributions. And without mentioning the sum which has been collected, I have every satisfaction in believing that it far exceeds one half of that which is annually offered. This is satisfactory in a pecuniary point of view, because it puts the Society in a position in which it may be more useful than it would have been if the contributions had been diminished, but the chief satisfaction which I feel is formed on a very different ground. It may be accepted as a proof that the feelings of the members of the Church of England throughout the Province, in favor of the Society, are not feelings which having been excited at the commencement of one year, necessarily lie dormant until the beginning of the next year: it shews that this society has struck its roots deeply into the hearts of the members of the church; that it has earned their gratitude, and they give it their confidence. Well then, I may believe, if I may so far anticipate, that the Report which you will hear will tell you, that at no previous part of its history was the Diocesan Church Society in so good a position as it is at the present moment. This is a subject for deep congratulation. But there is one point upon which

I wish to offer a remark before I close. It appears now that although the funds of the Church Society have been for many years increasing; and I believe they were never in so good a position previously to last year, as they were last year, and I believe that you will hear now that they are in a better position than they were at the commencement of the present year; yet at this moment, I regret to say, there are more missions unsupplied, more churches vacant, and greater difficulty in filling them than has been the case in former years. It is not a want of funds: if it were the members would supply them, but it arises from a very different cause, a cause which, in my opinion, deserves the attention and immediate care of every member of the church in the Province: *a paucity of clergymen.*

The Rev. W. Q. Ketchum, Secretary of the Society, then read the Report.

The Lord Bishop of Fredericton then moved* :—

Resolved, That the Report be received and printed under the direction of the Executive Committee.

Dr. Robb, in seconding the resolution, observed, that he felt it an honor to do so, inasmuch as this report was the formal summary of the evidence whereon churchmen in New Brunswick were moved and called upon to sustain the cause of the Diocesan Church Society. That evidence was satisfactory: the methods adopted to secure a succession of clergymen in the country had been well and wisely planned, and, no doubt, in due time every member of the church in the province would be a member of the Diocesan Church Society. The missionaries continued to report a growing interest in the cause of the church, a gradual extension of the means of grace in the way of the church, and increased offerings to its treasury. To common men the last appeared to be the best test of the goodness of the cause, and the proof that a blessing was with it. The cause was the cause of all who believed that they had immortal souls, and that in the Church of England there was a safe and sound guidance through the perils of the world to the peace of the realms beyond the grave. Hence the cause becomes a sacred one, and demands, on the part of the members of the church, their most earnest efforts. It was a duty incumbent upon all, and ought to be to all, more or less, a business. On the part of the old, there was required their highest wisdom; on the part of the middle aged, there was required their best energies; on the part of the young, their watchful attention and most ardent sympathies. Without this gradual training of the young to the business of the society, the society itself would fail. On referring to the Report of 1839, about the date of his first attendance on the meetings of the Church Society, he found there were of the clergy then present only two present here to-night, and of the lay delegates hardly even as many. The form of the Society indeed remained, but the active agents therein were gradually replaced, and so the work proceeded, and so only could it proceed. In support of the assertion that a blessing attended the cause, he observed that twenty years ago, that is, in the year above mentioned, the subscriptions amounted to about £400, while this year, the income of the society would not be less than £2,000. The foundations of the society had been at length broadly and deeply laid in the hearts of the members of the church, and judging from all the evidence just submitted to them, there was every reason to believe that for the next twenty years the rate of increase of the society's funds would be very much greater then even during the last. He repeated again that he felt himself greatly honored by being allowed to second the resolution so eloquently proposed by the Lord Bishop of the Diocese.

A. W. Savary, Esquire, in moving the second Resolution, viz.:

That the success vouchsafed to the Society at this its first anniversary meeting, under the late change in its Constitution, encourages the hope that, by the blessing of God, its sphere of usefulness may thereby be increased.

After humourously alluding to the emotions which he, although a lawyer,

* The Secretary of the Society has much reason to regret, that he failed in his endeavours to obtain a report of his Lordship's most impressive and valuable address.

experienced on rising in the metropolitan city to address a meeting of the Diocesan Church Society of New Brunswick for the first time, said, that while he was alive to the responsibility, he trusted he was not indifferent to the privilege of being permitted to take an humble part in the proceedings of such an occasion, proceedings the immediate object of which is the extension of scriptural knowledge, the diffusion of the Gospel, and that through the purest and holiest of all earthly channels—our evangelical and apostolic church. Moreover it is my pleasing duty to address you to-night in the language of congratulation, for I rise to move the resolution which has just been read. I have the more pleasure it doing so because the change referred to was always strenuously advocated by the rector of the parish (Dr. Gray) which I have the honor to represent; and whose absence from the meetings at this anniversary, with the valuable counsel and assistance which he always rendered, is, I am sure, a matter of general regret, as also the indisposition of bodily health by which that absence is occasioned.

The best evidence of success to which I can refer is, of course, to be found in the valuable and interesting report just read by the Secretary. This report however has already formed the subject of a distinct resolution, and it is my duty rather to trace the connection between the success to which it points, and the recent change in our Constitution, than to enter at large upon the various gratifying topics it embraces. Your Excellency expressed a belief that it would appear by the report that the subscriptions just taken up exceeded considerably half the amount of the annual collections made only six months ago. In reality they reach two thirds of that amount. And as we may fairly assume that those parishes not yet heard from will remit as large a proportion on their last annual subscription as the others have on theirs, I think the total contributions for the half year may be set down at very nearly £1100. This I think to be a most gratifying and convincing proof of a growing interest in the cause, and that the change in the constitution of the society is likely to be productive of great good. Could we reasonably estimate this contribution as strictly equivalent to a half yearly one—anticipating that at the annual collection twelve months hence the amount would be double, we might look forward to a revenue next year of over £2000. This, I am well aware, is too much to expect; but we will only require an advance of fifty per cent. to make the amount equal to that of the annual subscription six months ago; and considering how many have not been called upon, owing to the short period that elapsed between the two collections, and how many for the same reason have really given but half a subscription, and the fact that these returns only include the results of one collection in the respective churches, a rough estimate has convinced me that we may reasonably anticipate next year a far greater increase than fifty per cent. on the amount of these contributions. This amount therefore decidedly strengthens my conviction that the summer season, when the operations of our commerce are no longer impeded by the closing of navigation, when the industry of our people becomes productive, and money is more freely circulated in the community, will be found a much more convenient time than any other for bringing the claims of the society before the public. Objections may be easily answered. In any exceptional cases, the collections may still be made at periods the best adapted to success, under the circumstances of the particular locality.

But I must not forget what has been so well brought to our minds: our object is not simply the acquisition of funds; we do not propose to stop there; these are but means to an end, and that end must not be overlooked. We desire to strengthen and consolidate the Church of England in the hearts and affections of our people forever, and through its instrumentality to secure that most important of all ends, the salvation of souls. The zeal and fidelity of the missionaries it employs are the more immediate and efficient means for these purposes under the blessing of God. The usual statistics of their labors could not be embraced in this report; and therefore I cannot refer you to details; but I am sure that the Society has the fullest confidence that what we know them to have done in the past, they will have grace to continue in the future, and that success will abundantly crown their labors, under the blessing of God.

Perhaps I ought to advert to the fact that the attendance at these meetings has not been as large as usual. This is no proof that the change in the Constitution has not worked beneficially. Many of the clergy have been prevented from attending, owing to the near approach of the triennial visitation, and the inconvenience of leaving their parishes twice in so short a time; and many, both of the clergy and laity, doubtless considered these meetings as of much less importance than formerly, embracing only the business and appropriations of a half year, and that half year not to commence till the first of January next. Indeed, for this reason, we had no right to expect even *half* the usual attendance, and hence the number of those who *have* attended may be regarded as another proof of increasing interest in the cause.

But before I conclude, I will, with your Excellency's permission observe, that notwithstanding all we have yet accomplished, and the gratifying attachment of the members of our church generally throughout the diocese to this institution, much yet remains to be done, and a still livelier zeal ought yet to be awakened in its behalf. Few of us who have had anything to do with collecting its funds will deny that there are many who profess to recognize its claims, but do not follow up their professions by practical results; and there are many who meet our appeals for aid with cavils and excuses. One man will object that he has, "a family to support," feeling apparently but little of the solemn responsibility of Christians to provide for the religious as well as physical necessities of their offspring; to endeavour to leave behind them not solely an inheritance of earthly possessions, but those choicest of all blessings, only to be enjoyed by future generations through the instrumentality of a pure church established in the land. I have spoken of future generations: would that I had time to enter at large into the claims of such a society as this, in connexion with the future history of this country; its benefits not only in a religious, but in a philanthropic and patriotic point of view. Some allege that there are too many calls upon their charity; but I would like to know what call of charity churchmen ought to prefer to that which is addressed to them on behalf of the extension and endowment of their church, and of the various pious and holy objects which this society embraces. I cannot but believe that when the missionary work of the society is brought more prominently forward by the different local committees at public meetings, its claims to support will be far more cheerfully and universally responded to by the people. But as I understand this is to be the subject of another resolution, I will forbear further allusion to it, particularly as the advocacy of that resolution will engage the eloquence of the honourable Provincial Secretary, by whom no doubt the subject will be brought fully before us. I will only observe, that as these meetings would probably be held shortly before the general anniversary gatherings, they will occur under the change in the constitution, at the time when appeals on behalf of other kindred institutions are not generally made, and thus secure the more undivided attention and more liberal contributions of the public.

In conclusion, would that all of us might feel yet more and more impressed with our duty to aid with our means the holy objects we have assembled to promote. Oh! in view of the blessing which God will vouchsafe to the feeblest efforts properly made in His cause, how great is the error of those who withhold their contributions because they cannot afford sufficient to perform any notable good! The operations of grace, and the dispensations of Providence in His dealings with the church, are analogous to what we constantly observe in the natural world around us. The little rivulet that tracks its silent and unobtrusive way, scarcely perceptible amid the obscurity of the forest, and inaudible among the voices of nature, is destined to swell the volume of the river that expands over the plain. That river rolls on with a deeper and stronger current till it pours its tide into the mighty ocean that encircles the globe. And so the smallest contributions, flowing from the bounty of the humblest individual Christian into the channel of societies like these augment their influence and increase their efficiency: these again become tributaries and supplements to those grander institutions of christian benevolence and missionary enterprise which are the chief pride and ornament of our mother country, and embrace every region of the earth in the sphere of their operations, until all shall finally blend their sublime results in that "sea of glory" which shall "spread from pole to pole" when the glorious predictions of inspiration shall be accomplished, and "the earth shall be full of the knowledge of the glory of the Lord as the waters cover the sea."

The Rev. S. D. Lee Street, in seconding the Resolution said :—I am rather unwillingly placed in the position which I occupy this evening, but while advocating here as elsewhere the claims of the society, there are first one or two remarks which I shall make with reference to the change of time for holding the anniversary meeting. It has been urged as a great objection to this change, that during the winter season, when the members of the Legislature were present, there would be a greater facility afforded to obtain lay delegates to represent the various local committees: but, I trust, that the meeting this year has fully proved that *that* objection is groundless. Though, indeed, the meeting has not been as large as on former occasions, there are two reasons for that. It is but a short time since we were called together on an occasion similar to the present, and the clergy (and some of the *laity*, also, we hope) are shortly to assemble again at the call of the Lord Bishop for a triennial visitation. It would be inconvenient for the clergy to leave their parishes destitute on two occasions within so short a period of each other. There has been much said relative to the amount of the contributions, and what has been said has called my attention to the whole proceedings of the society from its commencement. If we trace it progress from year to year, and observe the increase not only of its means but of its usefulness, we cannot but be well convinced that God's blessing has attended it throughout, and this may be regarded as a sufficient guarantee of what may be accomplished by the continued and united exertions of churchmen of this Province. Much more might be effected by the increased zeal and liberality of each. When we take up the report of the society, and view the whole amount of annual contributions, taken as a whole, they shew a steady increase upon former years, and appear large and satisfactory. But when we view the subscriptions of individuals, we might almost take shame to ourselves at the smallness of them, with indeed the exception of a few generous gifts. I trust that now, when we have such increasing calls on the funds of our society, we shall become generally more alive to the necessity of increasing our contributions, to put the society in a position so that it may perform the work which is so urgent, and accomplish more than it has hitherto done. It has been remarked here this evening, by more than one speaker, that the great difficulty now to be met is a want of clergymen, but my opinion is that if there were sufficient means, it would not be long before men would be found ready to supply that want. If we have not men in this country, we may go to that Mother Country, whence we have received so much, through whose pecuniary aid the church here has been so long nourished, and through whose bounty also we have been supplied with men who are among the most zealous and energetic missionaries of the diocese. I fully trust, therefore, that if means were put into his Lordship's hands, he would be enabled to obtain a further supply to meet the present vacancies. To urge members of the church to larger contributions, I might here speak of the good done by the society; the missions sustained if not planted; the churches built; the parsonages erected; the books sent forth in their course of deep and silent instruction upon the principles of the church. We may be thankful to Almighty God for the benefits which have already arisen; but when we look upon the vast country before us, and think of what yet remains to be done, when we see the extensive settlements scattered throughout the country, with no holy man to administer to them, no one to baptize and teach their children, well may we say this is a double cause for greater exertions on behalf of this society. I may here particularly instance the country up the river St. John, between Woodstock and the Canada line, with extensive settlements on both sides of the river, yet throughout this wide domain there is but one solitary missionary, who with all the energy that man can give, is far from being able to supply even a small portion of that destitute part of the country. And this is but one of the many places all calling loudly for help: many of them the longer help is withheld, will be the more widely estranged from the church. In view of these things, we should all remember what our blessed Lord said to his disciples when they applied to Him for aid in behalf of the famishing multitudes in the wilderness. What He said to them, He now says to us who have enjoyed for so long a time the blessings and privileges of the Church, "Give ye them to eat." May we then, go hand in hand with united zeal in the good cause! I hope to see the day, when members from all parts of the country will not regard it as a great sacrifice of time, money, or anything else, to be present on these occasions; and being brought from every part of the Province, there would grow up greater unanimity of feeling and action, and a close and extended sympathy for each others wants and necessities. And as to the *amount* of their contributions, if men would but sacrifice one half of what they give to their luxuries, there would be no deficiency of means for the good work of the church.

The Hon. S. L. Tilley proposed the third Resolution, viz:—

That whereas the Missionary work of the Church is of such vast interest and importance, the Society would recommend, that this subject be brought more generally before its members at the annual meetings of the local committees, both with regard to the spiritual destitution of this Diocese, and also with reference to missions to heathen countries.

He said,—This resolution recognises the importance of the missionary work of the church, and recommends that the subject be brought prominently before the members of the society at the local general meetings; not only as regards the missionary work of this Diocese, but also as relates to heathen countries.

I may be permitted for a few moments, before entering directly upon the consideration of the resolution, to offer some observations relative to the changes which have recently been made in the constitution of the society; one of which has been referred to by the gentleman who moved the last resolution. I have invariably opposed the proposition to change the time for holding the general or anniversary meeting of the Society from a winter to a summer month. I did so because I feared, if the change was made, the attendance of the lay delegates from the various parishes would not be as numerous as heretofore, and the interest in the anniversary meeting would be somewhat diminished. The attendance this evening has in a great measure dispelled my fears on the latter point, and I sincerely hope that it may prove that my anticipations as regards the former were groundless.

The other change to which I refer, is the one by which the ordinary business of the society was transferred from the anniversary meeting to that of clerical and lay delegates, and the proceedings of the anniversary meeting confined to what has been termed platform speaking. This change has been highly beneficial. In former years, Your Excellency, and before you came to this country, the proceedings at our anniversary gatherings were necessarily, to a certain extent, uninteresting to a large number of those who attended them; but few felt interested in the discussions upon proposed amendments to our constitution, or the consideration of the propriety of a certain investment of our funds. The introduction of existing provisions afford us an opportunity, on these occasions, of speaking of the position and wants of our church, and how they are to be supplied; to remind ... h other of the privileges we enjoy, and the necessity that exi... ... ...boring to impart simila .. ...ngs to others; and in this way enc.. .ge e.. .imulate each other, th.. ..an we separate, it may be with a determination to do more than heretofore in the cause of our Redeemer, and for the extension of His Church. The anniversary meeting *now* affords a favourable opportunity for inculcating a missionary spirit—the object especially recommended by my resolution.

Let us, Your Excellency, consider the difficulties under which we labor, and what are the means to be adopted for their removal.

It has been correctly stated that we want both *men* and *money*. These can only be obtained by making our wants known in the proper quarter; first by prayer; secondly, by presenting the claims and the wants of our church to her members; and I consider the most effectual means for the accomplishment of this, is by calling them together in each parish, and, as my resolution recommends, there inculcating a thorough Missionary spirit. Were our wants known, and the necessities of our own diocese fully understood, the members of our church would, I doubt not, promptly meet them. Our present position is calculated to fill us with anxious cares for the future: we are compelled to vote our missionaries less than is sufficient to meet their real necessities, and with this division of the funds at our disposal, we cannot employ a sufficient number of missionaries to meet the claims made upon His Lordship. There are now three missions without clergymen, or the means to pay them, could their services be obtained, and we may reasonably expect that we will soon be called upon to provide for a considerable portion if not the whole of the sum now granted by the Society for the Propagation of the Gospel. These facts cannot be too strongly impressed upon churchmen. Discouraging as this state of things may appear, I repeat that the proper and earnest representation of these facts would produce the desired effect.

I will mention a circumstance by way of illustrating what might be done were proper means taken. When a resident in the parish of Portland, I was connected with the Sabbath School, and we were in the habit of distributing a Sunday School paper. One of these contained an appeal in behalf of a church and school in one of the Western States. This was read by the children, and it resulted in several of the scholars, the children of poor parents, bringing me sabbath after sabbath, the small sums received by them during the week, with a request that I would forward it to the proper party, in aid of the church and school referred to. More than a year after I left the parish, my successor informed me that these children still continued their contributions.

If then, Your Excellency, such an appeal, presented to children in behalf of a poor congregation in the neighbouring republic, produced such results, surely a similar appeal made general, and in behalf of the destitute in our own Diocese, would be cheerfully met by both children and parents. Such meetings should also be made available for supplying the other deficiency referred to, namely, clergymen. Parents should be urged to give their sons such an education as will enable them satifactorily to discharge their duties, should they feel a desire to labour in their Master's service, and these sons so educated, and the sons of churchmen generally, who feel an interest in the spiritual welfare of others, should be induced from the necessities of the case, as well as from a sense of duty, to devote themselves to the missionary work. In this way, our necessities may be met. After leaving the meeting last evening, I was depressed with the melancholy reflection, that from the lack of clergymen and the means to pay them, many members of our church must, for a time at least, be deprived of the Gospel privileges which they had recently enjoyed, and others of them continue far removed, as they have been for years, from these blessings.

When at the College to-day, to hear the oration delivered by the Principal, I could not but hope that some of the students there present might devote themselves to the work of the ministry, and that funds would be forthcoming, sufficient to sustain them in the missions now unhappily vacant.

It has been asserted, that if the Society for the Propagation of the Gospel were at some distant day to withdraw their grant, that the sum so withdrawn could not be provided in New Brunswick. I am prepared to admit that we might have some difficulty in providing for such an emergency, but I deny that the churchmen of New Brunswick are not *able* to meet the difficulty should it arrive. To prove this, I will suppose a case; and that is, that to-morrow, the price of flour should advance, say 8s. 9d. per barrel, and such advance above the amount we will require to pay, should continue for one year, would such an advance, even in this necessary of life, materially embarrass any member of our church. I think not. Still the additional expenditure to which the members of our church would be subjected during the year, would be not only equal to the sum received from the Society for the Propagation of the Gospel and the contributions to the Church Society, but would also be sufficient to provide eight or ten additional missionaries for the Province.

I concur with your Excellency and his Lordship, that the increased and increasing interest manifested in the society, as exhibited by an increase of contributions, is a subject of gratulation and thankfulness; but the question that we should ask ourselves on such an occasion is this, have we done all that we ought to have done, and might have done. I must confess for my own part, that the reflection which I have given this subject, has convinced me at least that I have not done all my duty in the matter. And when it is considered that the contributions of last year to the funds of the society, and they were larger than has been collected for any previous year, amount to but 7½d. for each member of the church in the diocese, I think this meeting will concur with me in the opinion, that our efforts have not been as great as the means at our disposal would warrrant. It is satisfactory to find that wherever missionary meetings have been held in the Province, there an increased interest is manifested in this society: it is emphatically a missionary society, and were an effort now made in this Province to obtain funds to support missionaries in the new fields now opening, for instance, in China, India and Japan, so far from such collections diminishing the amount that would otherwise be subscribed to this Society, I believe it would have a tendency to increase them. The man who would feel the necessity for contributing for the conversion of the heathen, would feel still more the necessity for providing for the destitute at home. We want more zeal, more love, and more self denial. These graces will be strengthened by meetings such as these. We have been so long aided by the Society for the Propagation of the Gospel that we have not felt the necessity for aiding this society. I can recollect when in some of our most wealthy parishes the members of the church paid nothing towards the support of the missionaries, and when called upon for 7s. 6d. or 10s. a year for pew rent, and this to keep the church in repair, it was considered a heavy tax. We are now, however, being better educated, and what we pay for we are the more likely to appreciate, and what we consider worth having, we will, if actuated by a christian spirit, desire that others should also possess.

Some five and twenty years since I read a verse or two, expressive of a churchman's love for and devotion to the church. I have not since forgotten them. The language is perhaps strong, but I could wish we could all make it our own. I will close my remarks by repeating them:

Then say, shall the Church, which our forefathers built,
Which the tempests of ages have battered in vain;
Abandoned by some from supineness or guilt,
O! say shall it fall by the vile and profane.
No! perish the impious hand that would take,
One shred from its altar, one stone from its towers;
The life's blood of martyrs has flown for its sake,
And its fall, if it fall, shall be reddened with ours.

The Rev. P. W. Loosemore, on rising to second the resolution, said: Although called upon somewhat unexpectedly by our respected Secretary to address you to night, I felt that I should be doing violence to my own feelings if I persisted in refusing to come forward in support of the cause of the Diocesan Church Society; especially at the present time, when, as we have been so ably and distinctly informed by his Lordship to-night, the church in this diocese is now about to be placed in a new and an untried, and we trust, we may add also, ladies and gentlemen, through your means and your influence, in a satisfactory and an independent position. The Hon. the Provincial Secretary has so ably and so eloquently set before you the claims of the resolution upon us, that it seems unnecessary for me to detain you with any prolonged observations, but I cannot content myself with merely *formally* seconding the resolution, nor sit down without saying a few words, to impress still further on the meeting the importance of the subject which the resolution conveys. It speaks of the destitute places of this Diocese, and as in times of old, Joshua and Caleb sent forth spies into the promised land, so now, in some such character as this, we go forth to the different and distant outlying districts, the back settlements and outposts of our extensive missions, and we come here this night, as it were, to head quarters, and repeat in the very same words, "there yet remaineth very much land to be possessed." There are fields to be cultivated, and fields "white already to the harvest," if we can only send forth laborers to put in the sickle; there are enemies to be dispossessed, and the rightful possessors of the soil to be implanted in their stead. It has been said to-night we have means sufficient. We *have* means sufficient for *present purposes*, but we require accumulated and accumulating means for the future maintenance and support of the church in this diocese, if it is to be maintained, as at present, in its integrity and efficiency.

With reference to the support which each member of the church should give to the great cause of the society, I was glad to hear from the Hon. the Provincial Secretary that such support should and might be very readily and properly increased, and hoping not at all to damage his remarks, but impress them more deeply upon you, I would call your attention to the first part of the resolution, which speaks of the spiritual destitution of this Diocese. We have been exhorted, "*freely* ye have received, freely give;" we have been told times without number, "he that soweth little shall reap little; and he that soweth plenteously shall reap plenteously. Let every man do according as he is disposed in his heart, not grudgingly or of necessity; for God loveth a cheerful giver." What is it to give freely, cheerfully, and not grudgingly? Every one has his own ideas about it, and the result of these the Hon. the Provincial Secretary has ably set forth to-night. That Book which alone gives us correct views upon every point, sets up a standard, which in these latter days has been lamentably overlooked. We refer not to-night to the *duty* of almsgiving, for that is a duty everywhere acknowledged, but we allude to the *standard* of almsgiving. Now, the Ceremonial Law, we say, has been abrogated or abolished, but the Moral Law stands firm for ever, and if one precept of that Moral Law be binding, so are all. I read, "Thou shalt truly tithe the increase of thy seed, that which the field bringeth forth to thee year by year;" and again, "the *tenth* shall be holy unto the Lord;" and again, St. Paul writing to the Hebrew Christians, says, "Even the patriarch Abraham gave to Melchizedec, the priest of the most High God, tithes of all." He gave the *tenth* of the spoils. And we maintain, that it is the *tenth* of our annual expenditure which the word of God requires us to devote to His cause and the cause of His church. It is not for us to decide whether any one, some, or all of the churchmen of this Diocese will be content to pay *tithes*, but this we are bound to do, to set up the standard, and to say, this is the work at which you are to aim; and whether it be for the general purposes of the Diocesan Church Society, or for the endowment of the church, or for any other church object, or for all, the *tithe* or *tenth* of our annual expenditure is the portion with which we are asked to "honor the Lord."

The second portion of the resolution refers to the missionary work of the church in the distant portions of the British Empire, in those vast heathen countries of Her Majesty's dominions on which the sun never sets. We know there is a vast missionary movement in the church, throughout the length and breadth of the land, answering to that mighty cry of the whole empire of heathendom, "Come over and help us." There are openings in China and Japan; openings in India; openings in Southern Africa, such as have been wholly unparalleled since the Gospel was first preached. It is impossible for me to give you anything like an adequate idea, within the limits of a single speech, of this vast missionary movement in the church, but I must point you to one portion of the great whole. We refer you to the chief Missionary College of the Church of England, the College of St. Augustine's, of Canterbury, founded in 1848, among whose missionaries, may it please your Excellency, your Excellency's humble servant has the honor to be enrolled. From almost every Diocese in England, there are now students at that College, and it is now sending forth its missionaries to almost every part of the world. It has its representatives in the island of Borneo, to go (we tell you as a fact, from personal knowledge), where the foot of the European has never before trod, and tell the land Dyak in his native mountain haunts, that there is a God who made him. It has its representatives in Capetown, to teach the Caffre, Zulu and Hottentot, to kneel at the foot of the Cross. It will have its representatives in India to confute the cunning Mahometan, the crafty Hindoo and the subtle Brahmin, in his own language, with his own arguments, and on his own ground; that is, to search for the seeds of truth which are to be found in those ancient and gigantic systems of error and superstition, to put them pre-eminently forward in the minds of the Hindoo, and to build upon them these fundamental doctrines of the Word of God, which are able to save the soul. It will have its representatives in China to tell the votaries of Confucius, Fo, and Buddha, the plain and simple story of the Cross; to teach the savage to live in comfort and happiness here below, and prepare for a joyful immortality. It has its representatives in New Brunswick, to add to and extend the church as here established in all its beauty, fulness and integrity.

It must be remembered and pressed upon you, that in proportion as each member of the church in this Diocese now comes forward, and according to his degree and measure, supplies the deficiency which is being caused by the withdrawal of the Society for the Propagation of the Gospel from this Diocese to send missionaries to heathen countries, in that proportion, it is not too much to say, will he be contributing to the mighty work of the regeneration of Africa, the conversion of China, and the evangelization of India.

Thoughts with reference to this subject crowd in upon my mind, which may be expressed in the borrowed words of an eloquent man, one of England's living preachers.

"The heart of the christian is sorrowful within him, as he thinks of the broad dominion of Paganism. He grieves over the rich and vast districts of the earth, inhabited only by the worshippers of idols, and is almost inclined to despair of the spread and triumph of the kingdom of Christ, so inveterate and deeply rooted appears the empire of Satan. But 'the idols he shall utterly abolish,' and nations long and even still oppressed with ignorance and superstition, shall receive the Gospel of Christ, and swell the ranks of His Church."

With these remarks, may it please your Excellency, I have the honor of seconding the resolution.

Moved by the Honorable Charles Fisher, Attorney General, seconded by W. Carman, Esquire.

That the following gentlemen be the officers of the Society for the current year :—W. J.

Bedell, Treasurer; Rev. W. Q. Ketchum, Secretary; W. H. Scovil and C. H. Fairweather, Auditors; and that the present members of the Executive Committee be re-elected for the period ending on the 1st Thursday in July next, viz.:—J. O. Allen, R. S. Armstrong, S. D. Berton, R. W. Crookshank, Jun., W. Carman, T. W. Daniel, George J. Dibblee, L. H. DeVeber, Joseph Henry Garbutt, R. F. Hazen, William Jack, J. Robb, M.D., J. M. Robinson, H. G. Simonds, Edward Simonds, Hon. J. A. Street, J. V. Thurgar, J. B. Toldervy, M.D., R. S. Thomson, J. Wilkinson, William Wright, J. W. Weldon, and Justus Wetmore.

His Excellency the Lieutenant Governor then left the chair, and on motion, the Right Rev. the Lord Bishop took the same, whereupon it was moved by the Hon. Mr. Justice Neville Parker, seconded by the Rev. C. Lee, and unanimously resolved—

That the thanks of the Society be tendered to His Excellency for his able and impartial conduct in the chair.

His Excellency acknowledged the resolution in the following terms:—

I must tender my most hearty acknowledgment to the Hon. Gentleman who moved this resolution, and to the meeting, who have sustained it, and to you, my Lord, for the terms in which you have conveyed it to me. It has been truly said, that it is my duty, in the position which I hold, to make no distinction of creeds—that duty, I hope, I have always performed. But the performance of that duty is not, in my opinion, inconsistent with the bold avowal of my personal attachment to the Church to which I belong; on the contrary, I believe, and my own experience has taught me that others, who may differ from me in opinion, have not the less respect for one who avows his own conscientious opinions *with charity.* You, my Lord, have been kind enough to say that I have given my humble assistance to support the Church, in my personal capacity, while I have been within the Province. I can truly say that such has been my endeavor. So far as attending at these meetings is concerned, I can also say, that if it has been a duty, it is a pleasant one, and it is more especially agreeable when, as on the present occasion, I have seen a spirit not only of union, but of *earnestness.* One idea has been expressed and shadowed forth by different speakers, under different forms, but it is the same idea throughout. And it is true, that the Church of England in this Province is a missionary church, and that when it asks for the assistance of churchmen, through the Diocesan Church Society, or any other means, it is not asking for *luxuries,* it is asking for *necessaries.* If this be a fact more and more realized among the churchmen of the Province, and if it be also known and felt that the appeal for contributions to the Church of England are not for luxuries, but for necessaries, then I shall agree with the Provincial Secretary, that there is no reason to fear for the Church of England in this Province.

The benediction was then pronounced by the Bishop, and the meeting separated.